Amelia Edith Huddleston Barr

A knight of the nets

Amelia Edith Huddleston Barr

A knight of the nets

ISBN/EAN: 9783742894359

Manufactured in Europe, USA, Canada, Australia, Japa

Cover: Foto ©Andreas Hilbeck / pixelio.de

Manufactured and distributed by brebook publishing software
(www.brebook.com)

Amelia Edith Huddleston Barr

A knight of the nets

A

KNIGHT OF THE NETS

BY

AMELIA E. BARR

NEW YORK

DODD, MEAD AND COMPANY

1896

CONTENTS.

Grey sky, brown waters: as a bird that flies
  My heart flits forth to these;
Back to the winter rose of Northern skies,
  Back to the Northern seas.

A KNIGHT OF THE NETS

CHAPTER I

THE WORLD SHE LIVED IN

IT would be easy to walk many a time through "Fife and all the lands about it" and never once find the little fishing village of Pittendurie. Indeed, it would be a singular thing if it was found, unless some special business or direction led to it. For clearly it was never intended that human beings should build homes where these cottages cling together, between sea and sky, — a few here, and a few there, hidden away in every bend of the rocks where a little ground could be levelled, so that the tides in stormy weather break with threat and fury on the very doorstones of the lowest cottages.

Yet as the lofty semicircle of hills bend inward, the sea follows; and there is a fair harbour, where the fishing boats ride together while their sails dry in the afternoon sun. Then the hamlet is very still; for the men are sleeping off the weariness of their night work, while the children play quietly among the tangle, and the women mend the nets or bait the lines for the next fishing. A lonely little spot, shut in by sea and land, and yet life is there in all its passionate variety — love and hate, jealousy and avarice, youth, with its ideal sorrows and infinite expectations, age, with its memories and regrets, and "sure and certain hope."

The cottages also have their individualities. Although they are much of the same size and pattern, an observing eye would have picked out the Binnie cottage as distinctive and prepossessing. Its outside walls were as white as lime could make them; its small windows brightened with geraniums and a white muslin curtain; and the litter of ropes and nets and drying fish which encumbered the majority of thatches, was pleasantly absent. Standing on a little level, thirty feet above the shingle, it faced the open sea, and was constantly filled with the confused tones of its sighing surges, and penetrated by its pulsating, tremendous vitality.

It had been the home of many generations of Binnies, and the very old, and the very young, had usually shared its comforts together; but at the time of my story, there remained of the family only the widow of the last proprietor, her son Andrew, and her daughter Christina. Christina was twenty years old, and still unmarried, — a strange thing in Pittendurie, where early marriages are the rule. Some said she was vain of her beauty and could find no lad whom she thought good enough; others thought she was a selfish, cold-hearted girl, feared for the cares and the labours of a fisherman's wife.

On this July afternoon, the girl had been some hours mending the pile of nets at her feet; but at length they were in perfect order, and she threw her arms upward and outward to relieve their weariness, and then went to the open door. The tide was coming in, but the children were still paddling in the salt pools and on the cold bladder rack, and she stepped forward to the edge of the cliff, and threw them some wild geranium and ragwort. Then she stood motionless in the bright sunlight, looking down the shingle towards the pier and the little tavern, from which came, in drowsy tones, the rough monotonous songs which seamen delight to sing — songs, full of the complaining of the sea, interpreted by the hoarse, melancholy voices of sea-faring men.

Standing thus in the clear light, her great beauty was not to be denied. She was tall and not too slender; and at this moment, the set of her head was like that of a thoroughbred horse, when it pricks its ears to listen. She had soft brown eyes, with long lashes and heavy eyebrows — eyes, reflecting the lances of light that darted in and out of the shifting clouds — an open air complexion, dazzling, even teeth, an abundance of dark, rippling hair, and a flush of ardent life opening her wide nostrils, and stirring gently the exquisite mould of her throat and bust. The moral impression she gave was that of a pure, strong, compassionate woman; cool-headed, but not cold; capable of vigorous joys and griefs.

After a few minutes' investigation, she went back to the cottage, and stood in the open doorway, with her head leaning against the lintel. Her mother had begun to prepare the evening meal; fresh fish were frying on the fire, and the oat cakes toasting before it. Yet, as she moved rapidly about, she was watching her daughter, and very soon she gave words to the thoughts troubling and perplexing her motherly speculations.

"Christina," she said, "you'll not require to be looking for Andrew. The lad is ben the house; he has been asleep ever since he eat his dinner."

"I know that, Mother."

"Well then, if it is Jamie Logan, let me tell

you it is a poor business. I have a fear and an inward down-sinking anent that young man."

"Perfect nonsense, Mother! There is nothing to fear you about Jamie."

"What good ever came through folk saved from the sea? Tell me that, Christina! They bring sorrow back with them. That is a fact none will deny."

"What could Andrew do but save the lad?"

"Why was the lad running before such a sea? He should have got into harbour; there was time enough. And if it was Andrew's duty to save him, it is not your duty to be loving him. You may take that much sense from me, anyway."

"*Whist, Mother!* He has not said a word of love to me."

"He perfectly changes colours every time he sees you, and why so, if it be not for love of you? I am not liking the look of the thing, Christina, and your brother is not liking it; and if you don't take care of yourself, you'll be in a burning fever of first love, and beyond all reasoning. Even now, you are making yourself a speculation to the whole village."

"Jamie is a straight-forward lad. I'm thinking he would lay his life down for me."

"I thought he had not said a word of love to you."

5

"A girl knows some things that are not told her."

"Very fine; but it will not be the fashion now to lie down and die for Annie Laurie, or any other lass. A young man who wants a wife must bustle around and get siller to keep her with. Getting married, these days is not a thing to make a song about. You are but a young thing yet, Christina, and you have much to learn."

"Would you not like to be young again, Mother?"

"No, I would not! I would not risk it. Besides, it would be going back; and I want to go forward and upward. But you need not try to turn the talk from Jamie Logan that way. I'll say again what I said before, you will be in a fever of first love, and not to be reasoned with, if you don't take care of yourself."

The girl flushed hotly, came into the house, and began to re-arrange the teacups with a nervous haste; for she heard Jamie's steps on the rocky road, and his voice, clear as a blackbird's, whistling gayly "In the Bay of Biscay O!"

"The teacups are all right, Christina. I am talking anent Jamie Logan. The lad is just a temptation to you; and you will require to ask for strength to be kept out of temptation; for

6

the Lord knows, the best of us don't expect strength to resist it."

Christina turned her face to her mother, and then left her answer to Jamie Logan. For he came in at the moment with a little tartan shawl in his hand, which he gallantly threw across the shoulders of Mistress Binnie.

"I have just bought it from a peddler loon," he said. "It is bonnie and soft, and it sets you well, and I hope you will pleasure me by wearing it."

His face was so bright, his manner so charming, that it was impossible for Janet Binnie to resist him. "You are a fleeching, flattering laddie," she answered; but she stroked and fingered the gay kerchief, while Christina made her observe how bright were the colours of it, and how neatly the soft folds fell around her. Then the door of the inner room opened, and Andrew came sleepily out.

"The fish is burning," he said, "and the oat cakes too; for I am smelling them ben the house;" and Janet ran to her fireside, and hastily turned her herring and cakes.

"I'm feared you won't think much of your meat to-night," she said regretfully; "the tea is fairly ruined."

"Never mind the meat, Mother," said Andrew. "We don't live to eat."

7

" Never mind the meat, indeed! What perfect nonsense! There is something wrong with folk that don't mind their meat."

" Well then, you should n't be so vain of yourself, Mother. You were preening like a young girl when I first got sight of you — and the meat taking care of itself."

" Me, vain! No! No! Nobody that knows Janet Binnie can ever say she is vain. I wot well that I am a frail, miserable creature, with little need of being vain, either for myself or my children. You are a great hand at arguing, Andrew, but you are always in the wrong. But draw to the table and eat. I'll warrant the fish will prove better than it is bonnie."

They sat down with a pleasant content that soon broadened into mirth and laughter, as Jamie Logan began to tell and to show how the peddler lad had fleeched and flethered the fisher wives out of their bawbees; adding at the last " that he could not come within sight of their fine words, they were that civil to him."

" Senselessly civil, no doubt of it," answered Janet. " A peddler aye gives the whole village a fit of the liberalities. The like of Jean Robertson spending a crown on him! Foolish woman, the words are not to seek that she'll get from me in the morning."

Then Jamie took a letter from his pocket,

and showed it to Andrew Binnie. " Robert Toddy brought it this morning," he said, " and, as you may see, it is from the firm of Henderson Brothers, Glasgow; and they say there will be a berth for me very soon now in one of their ships. And their boats are good, and their captains good, and there is chances for a fine sailor on that line. I may be a captain myself one of these days!" and he laughed so gayly, and looked so bravely into the face of such a bold idea, that he persuaded every one else to expect it for him. Janet pulled her new shawl a little closer and smiled, and her thought was: "After all, Christina may wait longer, and fare worse; for she is turned twenty." Yet she showed a little reserve as she asked: —

" Are you then Glasgow-born, Jamie? "

" Me! Glasgow-born! What are you thinking of? I am from the auld East Neuk; and I am glad and proud of being a Fifer. All my common sense comes from Fife. There is none loves the 'Kingdom' more than I, Jamie Logan. We are all Fife together. I thought you knew it."

At these words there was a momentary shadow across the door, and a little lassie slipped in; and when she did so, all put down their cups to welcome her. Andrew reddened to the roots of his hair, his eyes filled with light, a tender smile softened his firm mouth, and he put out his hand and drew the girl to the chair which Christina had pushed close to his own.

"You are welcome, and more than welcome, Sophy," said the Mistress; but for all that, she gave Sophy a glance in which there was much speculation not unmixed with fear and disapproval. For it was easy to see that Andrew Binnie loved her, and that she was not at all like him, nor yet like any of the fisher-girls of Pittendurie. Sophy, however, was not responsible for this difference; for early orphanage had placed her in the care of an aunt who carried on a dress and bonnet making business in Largo, and she had turned the little fisher-maid into a girl after her own heart and wishes.

Sophy, indeed, came frequently to visit her people in Pittendurie; but she had gradually grown less and less like them, and there was no wonder Mistress Binnie asked herself fearfully, "what kind of a wife at all Sophy would make for a Fife fisherman?" She was so small and genty, she had such a lovely face, such fair rippling hair, and her gown was of blue muslin made in the fashion of the day, and finished with a lace collar round her throat, and a ribbon belt round her slender waist.

" A bonnie lass for a carriage and pair,"
thought Janet Binnie; " but whatever will she do
with the creel and the nets? not to speak of
the bairns and the housework? "

Andrew was too much in love to consider
these questions. When he was six years old, he
had carried Sophy in his arms all day long; when
he was twelve, they had paddled on the sands,
and fished, and played, and learned their lessons
together. She had promised then to be his
wife as soon as he had a house and a boat of
his own; and never for one moment since had
Andrew doubted the validity and certainty of
this promise. To Andrew, and to Andrew's
family, and to the whole village of Pittendurie,
the marriage of Andrew Binnie and Sophy
Traill was a fact beyond disputing. Some said
" it was the right thing," and more said " it was
the foolish thing," and among the latter was
Andrew's mother; though as yet she had said it
very cautiously to Andrew, whom she regarded
as " clean daft and senselessly touchy about
the girl."

But she sent the young people out of the
house while she redd up the disorder made by
the evening meal; though, as she wiped her teacups, she went frequently to the little window,
and looked at the four sitting together on the
bit of turf which carpeted the top of the cliff

before the cottage. Andrew, as a privileged lover, held Sophy's hand; Christina sat next her brother, and facing Jamie Logan, so it was easy to see how her face kindled, and her manner softened to the charm of his merry conversation, his snatches of breezy sea-song, and his clever bits of mimicry. And as Janet walked to and fro, setting her cups and plates in the rack, and putting in place the tables and chairs, she did what we might all do more frequently and be the wiser for it — she talked to herself, to the real woman within her, and thus got to the bottom of things.

In less than an hour there began to be a movement about the pier, and then Andrew and Jamie went away to their night's work; and the girls sat still and watched the men across the level sands, and the boats hurrying out to the fishing grounds. Then they went back to the cottage, and found that Mistress Binnie had taken her knitting and gone to chat with a crony who lived higher up the cliff.

"We are alone, Sophy" said Christina; "but women folk are often that." She spoke a little sadly, the sweet melancholy of conscious, but unacknowledged love being heavy in her heart; and she would not have been sorry, had she been quite alone with her vaguely happy dreams. Neither of the girls was inclined to talk, but Christina wondered at Sophy's silence, for she had been unusually merry while the young men were present.

Now she sat quiet on the door step, clasping her left knee with little white hands that had no sign of labour on them but the mark of the needle on the left forefinger. At her side, Christina stood, her tall straight figure fittingly clad in a striped blue and white linsey petticoat, and a little josey of lilac print, cut low enough to show the white, firm throat above it. Her fine face radiated thought and feeling; she was on the verge of that experience which glorifies the simplest life. The exquisite glooming, the tender sky, the full heaving sea, were all in sweetest sympathy; they were sufficient; and Sophy's thin, fretful voice broke the charm and almost offended her.

"It is a weary life, Christina. How do you thole it?"

"You are just talking, Sophy. You were happy enough half an hour since."

"I was n't happy at all."

"You let on like you were. I should think you would be as fear'd to act a lie, as to tell one."

"I'll be going away from Pittendurie in the morning."

"What for?"

13

"I have my reasons."

"No doubt you have a 'because' of your own. But what will Andrew say? He is not expecting you to leave to-morrow."

"I don't care what Andrew says."

"Sophy Traill!"

"I don't. Andrew Binnie is not the whole of life to me."

"Whatever is the matter with you?"

"Nothing."

Then there was a pause, and Christina's thoughts flew seaward. In a few minutes, however, Sophy began talking again. "Do you go often into Largo, Christina?" she asked.

"Whiles, I take myself that far. You may count me up for the last year; for I sought you every time."

"Ay! Do you mind on the road a real grand house, fine and old, with a beautiful garden and peacocks in it — trailing their long feathers over the grass and gravel?"

"You will be meaning Braelands? Folks could not miss the place, even if they tried to."

"Well then, did you ever notice a young man around? He is always dressed for the saddle, or else he is in the saddle, and so most sure to have a whip in his hand."

"What are you talking about? What is the young man to you?"

" He is brawly handsome. They call him Archie Braelands."

" I have heard tell of him. And by what is said, I should not think he was an improving friend for any good girl to have."

" This, or that, he likes me. He likes me beyond everything."

" Do you know what you are saying, Sophy Traill? "

" I do, fine."

" Are you liking him? "

" It would not be hard to do."

" Has he ever spoke to you? "

" Well, he is not as shy as a fisher-lad. I find him in my way when I 'm not thinking. And see here, Christina; I got a letter from him this afternoon. A real love letter! Such lovely words! They are like poetry; they are as sweet as singing."

" Did you tell Andrew this? "

" Why would I do that? "

" You are a false little cutty, then. I would tell Andrew myself, but I am loath to hurt his true heart. Now you are to let Archie Braelands alone, or I will know the reason why."

" Preserve us all! What a blazing passion for nothing at all! Can't a lassie chat with a lad for a half hour without calling a court of sessions about it?" and she rose and shook out her dress, saying with an air of offence: —

"You may tell Andrew, if you like to. It would be a very poor thing if a girl is to be miscalled every time a man told her she was pretty."

"I'm not saying any woman can help men making fools of themselves; but you should have told Braelands that you were all the same as married, being promised so long to Andrew Binnie. And you ought to have told Andrew about the letter."

"Everybody can't live in Pittenduric, Christina. And if you live with a town full of folk, you cannot go up and down, saying to every man you meet, 'please, sir, I have a lad of my own, and you are not to cast a look at me, for Andrew Binnie would not like it.'"

"Hold your tongue, Sophy, or else know what you are yattering about. I would think shame to talk so scornful of the man I was going to marry."

"You can let it go for a passing remark. And if I have said anything to vex you, we are old friends, Christina, and it is not a lad that will part us. Sophy requires a deal of forgiving."

"She does," said Christina with a smile; "so I just forgive her as I go along, for she is still

16

doing something out of the way. But you must not treat Andrew ill. I could not love you, Sophy, if you did the like of that. And you must always tell me everything about yourself, and then nothing will go far wrong."

"Even that. I am not given to lying unless it is worth my while. I'll tell you aught there is to tell. And there is a kiss for Andrew, and you may say to him that I would have told him I was going back to Largo in the morning, only that I cannot bear to see him unhappy. That is a message to set him on the mast-head of pride and pleasure."

"I will give Andrew the kiss and the message, Sophy. And you take my advice, and keep yourself clear of that young Braelands. I am particular about my own good name, and I mean to be particular about yours."

"I have had your advice already, Christina."

"Well, this is a forgetful world, so I just mention the fact again."

"All the same, you might remember, Christina, that there was once a woman who got rich by minding her own business;" and with a laugh, the girl tied her bonnet under her chin, and went swiftly down the cliff towards the village.

CHAPTER II

CHRISTINA AND ANDREW

THIS confidence greatly troubled Christina; and as Sophy crossed the sands and vanished into the shadows beyond, a strange, sad presentiment of calamity oppressed her heart. Being herself in the enthusiasm of a first love, she could not conceive such treachery possible as Sophy's word seemed to imply. The girl had always been petted, and yet discontented with her situation; and had often made complaints which had no real foundation, and which in brighter moods she was likely to repudiate. And this night Andrew, instead of her Aunt Kilgour, was the object of her dissatisfaction — that would be all. To-morrow she would be complaining to Andrew of her aunt's hard treatment of her, and Andrew would be whispering of future happiness in her ears.

Upon the whole, therefore, Christina thought it would be cruel and foolish to tell her brother a word of what Sophy had said. Why should she disturb his serene faith in the girl so dear to him, until there was some more evident reason to do so? He was, as his mother said, " very touchy" about Sophy, being well aware that the village did not approve of the changes in her dress, and of those little reluctances and reserves in her behaviour, which had sprung up inevitably amid the refinements and wider acquaintances of town life.

"And so many things happen as the clock goes round," she thought. " Braclands may say or do something that will put him out of favour. Or he may take himself off to a foreign country — he is gey fond of France and Germany too — and Goodness knows! he will never be missed in Fifeshire. Or *them behind* may sort what flesh and blood cannot manage; so I will keep a close mouth anent the matter. One may think what one dare not say; for words, once spoken, cannot be wiped out with a sponge — and more 's the pity!"

Christina had also reached a crisis in her own life, — a crisis so important, that it quite excused the apparent readiness with which she dismissed Sophy's strange confidence. For the feeling between Jamie Logan and herself had grown to expression, and she was well aware that what had hitherto been in a large measure secret and private to themselves, had this night become evident to others. And she was not sure how

Jamie would be received. Andrew had saved his life in a sudden storm, and brought him to the Binnie cottage until he should be able to return to his own place. But instead of going away, he had hired his time for the herring season to a Pittendurie fisherman; and every spare hour had found him at the Binnie cottage, wooing the handsome Christina.

The village was not unanimously in his favour. No one could say anything against Jamie Logan; but he was a stranger, and that fact was hard to get over. A man must serve a very strict and long probation to be adopted into a Fife fishing community, and it was considered " very upsetting " for an unkent man to be looking up to the like of Christina Binnie, — a lass whose forbears had been in Pittendurie beyond the memory or the tradition of its inhabitants.

Janet also was not quite satisfied; and Christina knew this. She expected her daughter to marry a fisherman, but at least one who owned his share in a good boat, and who had a house to take a wife to. This strange lad was handsome and good-tempered; but, as she reflected, and not unfrequently said, " good looks and a laugh and a song, are not things to lippen to for house-keeping." So, on the whole, Christina had just the same doubts and anxieties as might trouble a fine lady of family and wealth, who had fallen in love with some handsome fellow whom her relatives were uncertain about favouring.

A week after Sophy's visit, however, Jamie found the unconquerable hour in which every true love comes to its blossoming. It was the Sabbath night, and a great peace was over the village. The men sat at their doors talking in monosyllables to their wives and mates; the children were asleep; and the full ocean breaking and tinkling upon the shingly coast. They had been at kirk together in the afternoon, and Jamie had taken tea with the Binnies after the service. Then Andrew had gone to see Sophy, and Janet to help a neighbour with a sick husband; so Jamie, left with Christina, had seized gladly his opportunity to teach her the secret of her own heart.

Sitting on the lonely rocks, with the moonlit sea at their feet, they had confessed to each other how sweet it was to love. And the plans growing out of this confession, though humble enough, were full of strange hope and happy dreaming to Christina. For Jamie had begged her to become his wife as soon as he got his promised berth on the great Scotch line, and this event would compel her to leave Pittendurie and make her home in Glasgow, — two facts, simply stupendous to the fisher-girl, who had never been twenty miles from her home, and to whom all life outside the elementary customs of Pittenduric was wonderful and a little frightsome.

But she put her hand in Jamie's hand, and felt his love sufficient for whatever love might bring or demand. Any spot on earth would be heaven to her with him, and for him; and she told him so, and was answered as women love to be answered, with a kiss that was the sweetness and confidence of all vows and promises. Among these simple, straight-forward people, there are no secrecies in love affairs; and the first thing Jamie did was to return to the cottage with Christina to make known the engagement they had entered into.

They met Andrew on the sands. He had been disappointed. Sophy had gone out with a friend, and her aunt had seemed annoyed and had not asked him to wait. He was counting up in his mind how often this thing had happened lately, and was conscious of an unhappy sense of doubt and unkindness which was entirely new to him. But when Christina stepped to his side, and Jamie said frankly, " Andrew, your dear sweet sister loves me, and has promised to be my wife, and I hope you will give us the love and favour we are seeking," Andrew looked tenderly into his sister's face, and their smiles met and seemed to kiss each other. And he took her hand between his own hands, and then put it into Jamie's.

"You shall be a brother to me, Jamie," he said; "and we will stand together always, for the sake of our bonnie Christina." And Jamie could not speak for happiness; but the three went forward with shining eyes and linked hands, and Andrew forgot his own fret and disappointment, in the joy of his sister's betrothal.

Janet came home as they sat in the moonlight outside the cottage. "Come into the house," she cried, with a pretense of anger. "It is high time for folk who have honest work for the morn to be sleeping. What hour will you get to the week's work, I wonder, Christina? If I leave the fireside for a minute or two, everything stops but daffing till I get back again. What for are you sitting so late?"

"There is a good reason, Mother," said Andrew, as he rose and with Jamie and Christina went into the cottage. "Here is our Christina been trysting herself to Jamie, and I have been giving them some good advice."

"Good advice!" laughed Janet. "Between you and Jamie Logan, it is the blind leading the blind, and nothing better. One would think there was no other duty in life than trysting and marrying. I have just heard tell of Flora Thompson and George Buchan, and now it is

Christina Binnie and Jamie Logan. The world is given up, I think, to this weary lad and lass business."

But Janet's words belied her voice and her benign face. She was really one of those delightful women who are " easily persuaded," and who readily accept whatever is, as right. For she had naturally one of the healthiest of human souls; besides which, years had brought her that tender sagacity and gentleness, which does not often come until the head is gray and the brow furrowed. So, though her words were fretful, they were negatived by her beaming smile, and by the motherly fashion in which she drew Christina to her side and held out her hand to Jamie.

"You are a pair of foolish bairns," she said; "and you little know what will betide you both."

" Nothing but love and happiness, Mother," answered Jamie.

" Well, well! look for good, and have good. I will not be one to ask after evil for you. But mind one thing, Jamie, you are marrying a woman, and not an angel. And, Christina, if you trust to any man, don't expect over much of him; the very best of them will stumble once in a while."

Then she drew forward the table, and put on the kettle and brewed some toddy, and set it out with toasted cake and cheese, and so drank, with cheerful moderation, to the health and happiness of the newly-promised lovers. And afterwards "the books" were opened, and Andrew, who was the priest of the family, asked the blessing of the Infinite One on all its relationships. Then the happiness that had been full of smiles and words became too deep for such expression; and they clasped hands and kissed each other "good night" in a silence, that was too sweetly solemn and full of feeling for the translation of mere language.

Before the morning light, Mistress Binnie had fully persuaded herself that Christina was going to make an unusually prosperous marriage. All her doubts had fled. Jamie had spoken out like a man; he had the best of prospects, and the wedding was likely to be something beyond a simple fisherman's bridal. She could hardly wait until the day's work was over, and the evening far enough advanced for a gossiping call on her crony, Marget Roy. Last night she had fancied Marget told her of Flora Thompson's betrothal with an air of pity for Christina; there was now a delightful retaliation in her power. But she put on an expression of dignified resignation, rather than one of pleasure, when she made known the fact of Christina's approaching marriage.

"I am glad to hear tell of it," said Marget frankly. "Christina will make a good wife, and she will keep a tidy house, I'll warrant her."

"She will, Marget. And it is a very important thing; far more so than folks sometimes think. You may put godliness into a woman after she is a wife, but you can not put cleanliness; it will have to be born in her."

"And so Jamie Logan is to have a berth from the Hendersons? That is far beyond a place in Lowrie's herring boats."

"I'm thinking he just stopped with Lowrie for the sake of being near-by to Christina. A lad like him need not have spent good time like that."

"Well, Janet, it is a good thing for your Christina, and I am glad of it."

"It is;" answered Janet, with a sigh and a smile. "The lad is sure to get on; and he's a respectable lad — a Fifer from Kirkcaldy — handsome and well-spoken of; and I am thinking the *Line* has a big bargain in him, and is proud of it. Still, I'm feared for my lassie, in such an awful, big, wicked-like town as Glasgow."

"She'll not require to take the whole town in. She will have her Bible, and her kirk, and her own man. There is nothing to fear you. Christina has her five senses."

CHRISTINA AND ANDREW

"No doubt. And she is to have a floor of her own and all things convenient; so there is comfort and safety in the like of that."

"What for are you worrying yourself then?"

"There's contingencies, Marget, — contingencies. And you know Christina is my one lassie, and I am sore to lose her. But 'lack a day! we cannot stop the clock. And marriage is like death — it is what we must all come to."

"Well Janet, your Christina has been long spared from it. She'll be past twenty, I'm thinking."

"Christina has had her offers, Marget. But what will you? We must all wait for the right man, or go to the de'il with the wrong one."

Thus the conversation went on, until Janet had exhausted all the advantages and possibilities that were incident to Christina's good fortune. And perhaps it was out of a little feeling of weariness of the theme, that Marget finally reminded her friend that she would be "lonely enough wanting her daughter," adding, "I was hearing too, that Andrew is not to be kept single much longer; and it will be what no one expects if Sophy Traill ever fills Christina's shoes."

"Sophy is well enough," answered Janet with a touch of pride. "She suits Andrew, and it is Andrew that has to live with her."

27

"And you too, Janet?"

"Not I! Andrew is to build his own bigging. I have the life rent of mine. But I shall be a deal in Glasgow myself. Jamie has his heart fairly set on that."

She made this statement with an air of prideful satisfaction that was irritating to Mistress Roy; and she was not inclined to let Janet enter anew into a description of all the fine sights she was to see, the grand guns of preachers she was to hear, and the trips to Greenock and Rothesay, which Jamie said "would just fall naturally in the way of their ordinary life." So Marget showed such a hurry about her household affairs as made Janet uncomfortable, and she rose with a little offence and said abruptly: —

"I must be going. I have the kirkyard to pass; and between the day and the dark it is but a mournful spot."

"It is that," answered Marget. "Folks should not be on the road when the bodiless walk. They might be in their way, and so get ill to themselves."

"Then good night, and good befall you;" but in spite of the benediction, Janet felt nettled at her friend's sudden lack of interest.

"It was a spat of envy no doubt," she thought; "but Lord's sake! envy is the most insinuating vice of the lot of them. It cannot behave itself for an hour at a time. But I'm not caring! it is better to be envied than pitied."

These reflections kept away the thought and fear of the " bodiless," and she passed the kirk-yard without being mindful of their proximity; the coming wedding, and the inevitable changes it would bring, filling her heart with all kinds of maternal anxieties, which in solitude would not be put aside for all the promised pride and *éclat* of the event. As she approached the cottage, she met Jamie and Christina coming down the cliff-side together, and she cried, " Is that you, Jamie?"

"As far as I know, it's myself, Mother," answered Jamie.

" Then turn back, and I'll get you a mouth-ful of bread and cheese. You'll be wanting it, no doubt; for love is but cold porridge to a man that has to pull on the nets all night."

" You have spoken the day after the fair, Mother," answered Jamie. "Christina has looked well to me, and I am bound for the boats."

" Well, well, your way be it."

Then Christina turned back with her mother, and they went silently back to the cottage, their hearts being busy with the new hopes and happiness that had come into their hitherto uneventful lives. But reticence between this mother and daughter was not long possible; they were too much one to have reserves; and neither being sleepy, they soon began to talk over again what they had discussed a hundred times before — the wedding dress, and the wedding feast, and the napery and plenishing Christina was to have for her own home. They sat on the hearth, before the bit of fire which was always necessary in that exposed and windy situation; but the door stood open, and the moon filled the little room with its placid and confidential light. So it is no wonder, as they sat talking and vaguely wondering at Andrew's absence, Christina should tell her mother what Sophy had said about Archie Braelands.

Janet listened with a dour face. For a moment she was glad; then she lifted the poker, and struck a block of coal into a score of pieces, and with the blow scattered the unkind, selfish thoughts which had sprung up in her heart.

"It is what I expected," she answered. "Just what I expected, Christina. A lassie dressed up in muslin, and ribbons, and artificial roses, isn't the kind of a wife a fisherman wants — and sooner or later, like goes to like. I am not blaming Sophy. She has tried hard to be faithful to Andrew, but what then? Nothing happens for nothing; and it will be a good thing for Andrew if Sophy leaves him; a good thing for Sophy too, I'm thinking; and better *is* better, whatever comes or goes."

" But Andrew will fret himself sorely."

" He will; no doubt of that. But Andrew has a good heart, and a good heart breaks bad fortune. Say nothing at all to him. He is wise enough to guide himself; though God knows! even the wisest of men will have a fool in his sleeve sometimes."

" Would there be any good in a word of warning? Just to prepare him for the sorrow that is on the road."

" There would be no sense in the like of it. If Andrew is to get the fling and the buffet, he will take it better from Sophy than from any other body. Let be, Christina. And maybe things will take a turn for the dear lad yet. Hope for it anyhow. Hope is as cheap as despair."

" Folks will be talking anon."

" They are talking already. Do you think that I did not hear all this clash and clavers before? Lucky Sims, and Marget Roy, and every fish-wife in Pittendurie, know both the beginning and the end of it. They have seen this, and they have heard that, and they think the very worst that can be; you may be sure of that."

" I 'm thinking no wrong of Sophy."

" Nor I. The first calamity is to be born a woman; it sets the door open for every other sorrow — and the more so, if the poor lassie is bonnie and alone in the world. Sophy is not to blame; it is Andrew that is in the fault."

" How can you say such a thing as that, Mother?"

" I 'll tell you how. Andrew has been that set on having a house for his wife, that he has just lost the wife while he was saving the siller for the house. I have told him, and better told him to bring Sophy here; but nothing but having her all to himself will he hear tell of. It is pure, wicked selfishness in the lad! He simply cannot thole her to give look or word to any one but himself. Perfect scand'lous selfishness! That is where all the trouble has come from."

" *Whist, Mother!* He is most at the doorstep. That is Andrew's foot, or I am much mista'en."

" Then I 'll away to Lizzie Robertson's for an hour. My heart is knocking at my lips, and I 'll be saying what I would give my last bawbee to unsay. Keep a calm sough, Christina."

" You need not tell me that, Mother."

" Just let Andrew do the talking, and you 'll be all right. It is easy to put him out about

Sophy, and then to come to words. Better keep peace than make peace."

She lifted the stocking she was knitting, and passed out of one door as Andrew came in at the other. He entered with that air of strength and capability so dear to the women of a household. He had on his kirk suit, and Christina thought, as he sat down by the open window, how much handsomer he looked in his blue guernsey and fishing cap.

" You'll be needing a mouthful and a cup of tea, Andrew?" she asked.

Andrew shook his head and answered pleasantly, " Not I, Christina. I had my tea with Sophy. Where is mother?"

" She is gone to Lizzie Robertson's for an hour. Her man is yet very badly off. She said she would sit with him till the night turned. Lizzie is most worn out, I 'm sure, by this time."

" Where is Jamie?"

" He said he was going to the fishing. He will have caught his boat, or he would have been back here again by this hour."

" Then we are alone? And like to be for an hour? eh, Christina?"

" There will be no one here till mother comes at the turn of the night. What for are you asking the like of them questions, Andrew?"

" Because I have been seeking this hour. I

3   33

have things to tell you, Christina, that must never go beyond yourself; no, not even to mother, unless the time comes for it. I am not going to ask you to give me your word or promise. You are Christina Binnie, and that is enough."

"I should say so. The man or woman who promises with an oath is not to be trusted. There is you and me, and God for our witness. What ever you have to say, the hearer and the witness is sufficient."

"I know that. Christina, I have been this day to Edinburgh, and I have brought home from the bank six hundred pounds."

"Six hundred pounds, Andrew! It is not believable."

"*Whist, woman!* I have six hundred pounds in my breast pocket, and I have siller in the house beside. I have sold my share in the 'Sure-Giver,' and I have been saving money ever since I put on my first sea-boots."

"I have always thought that saving money was your great fault, Andrew."

"I know. I know it myself only too well. Many's the Sabbath day I have been only a bawbee Christian, when I ought to have put a shilling in the plate. But I just could not help it."

"Yes, you could."

"Tell me how, then."

34

" Just try and believe that you are putting your collection into the hand of God Almighty, and not into a siller plate. Then you will put the shilling down and not the bawbee."

"Perhaps. The thought is not a new one to me, and often I have forced myself to give a white shilling instead of a penny-bit at the kirk door, just to get the better of the de'il once in a while. But for all that I know right well that saving siller is my besetting sin. However, I have been saving for a purpose, and now I am most ready to take the desire of my heart."

" It is a good desire; I am sure of that, Andrew."

" I think it is; a very good one. What do you say to this? I am going to put all my siller in a carrying steamer — one of the Red-White fleet. And more to it. I am to be skipper, and sail her from the North Sea to London."

" Will she be a big boat, Andrew? "

" She will carry three thousand ' trunks ' of fish in her ice chambers. What do you think of that? "

" I am perfectly dazzled and dumbfoundered with the thought of it. You will be a man of some weight in the world, when that comes to pass."

" I will be Captain Binnie, of the North Sea fleet, and Sophy will have reason enough for her

35

muslins, and ribbons, and trinkum-trankums —
God bless her!"

"You are a far forecasting man, Andrew."

"I have been able to clear my day and my
way, by the help of Providence, so far," said
Andrew, with a pious reservation; "just as my
decent kirk-going father was before me. But
that is neither here nor there, and please God, .
this will be a monumental year in my life."

"It will that. To get the ship and the wife
you want, within its twelve bounds, is a blessing
beyond ordinary. I am proud to hear tell of
such good fortune coming your way, Andrew."

"Ay; I knew you would. But I have the
siller, and I have the skill, and why should n't I
lift myself a bit?"

"And Sophy with you? Sophy will be an
ornament to any place you lift her to. And
you may come to own a fishing fleet yourself
some day, Andrew!"

"I am thinking of it," he answered, with the
air of a man who feels himself master of his
destiny. "But come ben the house with me,
Christina. I have something to show you."

So they went together into an inner room, and
Andrew moved aside a heavy chest of drawers
which stood against the wall. Then he lifted a
short plank beneath them, and putting his arm
far under the flooring, he pulled forth a tin box.

The key to it was in the leather purse in his breast pocket, and there was a little tantalizing delay in its opening. But when the lid was lifted, Christina saw a hoard of golden sovereigns, and a large roll of Bank of England bills. Without a word Andrew added the money in his pocket to this treasured store, and in an equal silence the flooring and drawers were replaced; and then, without a word, the brother and sister left the room together.

There was however a look of exultation on Christina's face, and when Andrew said " You understand now, Christina? " she answered in a voice full of tender pride.

" I have seen. And I am sure that Andrew Binnie is not the man to be moving without knowing the way he is going to take."

" I am not moving at all, Christina, for three months or perhaps longer. The ship I want is in dry dock until the winter; and it is all this wealth of siller that I am anxious about. If I should go to the fishing some night, and never come back, it would be the same as if it went to the bottom of the sea with me, not a soul but myself knowing it was there."

" But not now, Andrew. You be to tell me what I am to do if the like of that should happen; and your wish will be as the law of God to me."

37

"I am sure of that, Christina. Take heed then. If I should go out some night and the sea should get me, as it gets many better men, then you will lift the flooring, and take the money out of hiding. And you will give Sophy Traill one half of all there is. The other half is for mother and yourself. And you will do no other way with a single bawbee, or the Lord will set His face against it."

"I will do just what you tell me."

"I know it. To think different, would be just incredible nonsense. That is for the possibilities, Christina. For the days that are coming and going, I charge you, Christina Binnie, never to name to mortal creature the whereabouts of the money I have shown you."

"Your words are in my heart, Andrew. They will never pass my lips."

"Then that is enough of the siller. I have had a happy day with Sophy, and O the grace of the lassie! And the sweet innocence and lovesomeness of her pretty ways! She is budding into a very rose of beauty! I bought her a ring with a shining stone in it, and a gold brooch, and a bonnie piece of white muslin with the lace for the trimming of it; and the joy of the little beauty set me laughing with delight. I would not call the Queen my cousin, this night."

"Sophy ought to love you with all her heart and soul, Andrew."

"She does. She has arled her heart and hand to me. I thank *The Best* for this great mercy."

"And you can trust her without a doubt, dear lad?"

"I have as much faith in Sophy Traill, as I have in my Bible."

"That is the way to trust. It is the way I trust Jamie. But you'll mind how ready bad hearts and ill tongues are to give you a sense of suspicion. So you'll not heed a word of that kind, Andrew?"

"Not one. The like of such folk cannot give me a moment's trouble — there was Kirsty Johnston — "

"You may put Kirsty Johnston, and all she says to the wall."

"I'm doing it; but she called after me this very evening, 'take care of yourself, Andrew Binnie.' 'And what for, Mistress?' I asked. 'A beauty is hard to catch and worse to keep,' she answered; and then the laugh of her! But I didn't mind it, not I; and I didn't give her word or look in reply; for well I know that women's tongues cannot be stopped, not even by the Fourth Commandment."

Then Andrew sat down and was silent, for a

happiness like his is felt, and not expressed. And Christina moved softly about, preparing the frugal supper, and thinking about her lover in the fishing boats, until, the table being spread, Andrew drew his chair close to his sister's chair, and spreading forth his hands ere he sat down, said solemnly: —

"*This is the change of Thy Right Hand, O Thou Most High! Thou art strong to strengthen; gracious to help; ready to better; mighty to save. Amen!*"

It was the prayer of his fathers for centuries — the prayer they had used in all times of their joy and sorrow; the prayer that had grown in his own heart from his birth, and been recorded for ever in the sagas of his mother's people.

CHAPTER III

THE AILING HEART

NOT often in her life had Christina felt so happy as she did at this fortunate hour. Two things especially made her heart sing for joy; one was the fact that Jamie had never been so tender, so full of joyful anticipation, so proud of his love and his future, as in their interview of that evening. The very thought of his beauty and goodness made her walk unconsciously to the door, and look over the sea towards the fish-ing-grounds, where he was doubtless working at the nets, and thinking of her. And next to this intensely personal cause of happiness, was the fact that of all his mates, and even before his mother or Sophy, Andrew had chosen *her* for his confidant. She loved her brother very much, and she respected him with an equal fervour. Few men, in Christina's opinion, were able to stand in Andrew Binnie's shoes, and she felt, as she glanced at his strong, thoughtful face, that he was a brother to be very proud of.

He sat on the hearth with his arms crossed above his head, and a sweet, grave smile irradiating his strong countenance. Christina knew that he was thinking of Sophy, and as soon as she had spread the frugal meal, and they had sat down to their cakes and cheese, Andrew began to talk of her. He seemed to have dismissed absolutely the thought of the hidden money, and to be wholly occupied with memories of his love. And as he talked of her, his face grew vivid and tender, and he spoke like a poet, though he knew it not.

" She is that sweet, Christina, it is like kissing roses to kiss her. Her wee white hand on my red face is like a lily leaf. I saw it in the looking-glass, as we sat at tea. And the ring, with the shining stone, set it finely. I am the happiest man in the world, Christina! "

" I am glad with all my heart for you, Andrew, and for Sophy too. It is a grand thing to be loved as you love her."

"She is the sweetness of all the years that are gone, and of all that are to come."

" And Sophy loves you as you love her? I hope she does that, my dear Andrew."

" She will do. She will do! no doubt of it, Christina! She is shy now, and a bit frighted at the thought of marriage — she is such a gentle little thing — but I will make her love me ; yes I will! I will make her love me as I love her. What for not?"

42

"To be sure. Love must give and take equal, to be satisfied. I know that myself. I am loving Jamie just as he loves me."

" He is a brawly fine lad. Peddie was saying there was n't a better worker, nor a merrier one, in the whole fleet."

" A good heart is always a merry one, Andrew."

" I 'm not doubting it."

Thus they talked with kind mutual sympathy and confidence; and a certain sweet serenity and glad composure spread through the little room, and the very atmosphere was full of the peace and hope of innocent love. But some divine necessity of life ever joins joy and sorrow together; and even as the brother and sister sat speaking of their happiness, Christina heard a footstep that gave her heart a shock. Andrew was talking of Sophy, and he was not conscious of Jamie's approach until the lad entered the house. His face was flushed, and there was an air of excitement about him which Andrew regarded with an instant displeasure and suspicion. He did not answer Jamie's greeting, but said dourly: —

" You promised to take my place in the boat to-night, Jamie Logan ; then what for are you here, at this hour? I see one thing, and that is, you cannot be trusted to."

"I deserve a reproof, Andrew, for I have

43

earned it," answered Jamie; and there was an air of candid regret in his manner which struck Christina, but which was not obvious to Andrew as he added, "I'll not lie to you anent the matter."

"You need n't. Nothing in life is worth a lie."

"That may be, or not be. But it was just this way. I met an old friend as I was on my way to the boat, and he was poor, and hungry, and thirsty, and I be to take him to the 'public,' and give him a bite and a sup. Then the whiskey set us talking of old times and old acquaintances, and I clean forgot the fishing ; and the boats went away without me. And that is all there is to it."

"Far too much! Far too much! A nice lad you will be to trust to in a big ship full of men and women and children! A glass of whiskey, and a crack in the public house, set before your promised word and your duty! How will I trust Christina to you? When you make Andrew Binnie a promise, he expects you to keep it. Don't forget that! It may be of some consequence to you if you are wanting his sister for a wife."

With these words Andrew rose, went into his own room without a word of good-night, and with considerable show of annoyance, closed and bolted the door behind him. Jamie sat down by Christina, and waited for her to speak.

But it was not easy for her to do so. Try as she would, she could not show him the love she really felt. She was troubled at his neglect of duty, and so sorry that he, of all others, should have been the one to cast the first shadow across the bright future which she had been anticipating before his ill-timed arrival. It was love out of time and season, and lacked the savour and spontaneity which are the result of proper conditions. Jamie felt the unhappy atmosphere, and was offended.

"I 'm not wanted here, it seems," he said in a tone of injury.

"You are wanted in the boat, Jamie; that is where the fault lies. You should have been there. There is no outgait from that fact."

"Well then, I have said I was sorry. Is not that enough?"

"For me, yes. But Andrew likes a man to be prompt and sure in business. It is the only way to make money."

"Make money! I can make money among Andrew Binnie's feet, for all he thinks so much of himself. A friend's claims are before money-making. I 'll stand to that, till all the seas go dry."

"Andrew has very strict ideas; you must have found that out, Jamie, and you should not go against them."

"Andrew is headstrong as the north-wind. He goes clear o'er the bounds both sides. Everything is the very worst, or the very best. I'm not denying I was a bit wrong, but I consider I had a good excuse for it."

"Is there ever a good excuse for doing wrong, Jamie? But we will let the affair drop out of mind and talk. There are pleasanter things to speak of, I'm sure."

But the interview was a disappointment. Jamie went continually back to Andrew's reproof, and Christina herself seemed to be under a spell. She could not find the gentle words that would have soothed her lover, her manner became chill and silent; and Jamie finally went away, much hurt and offended. Yet she followed him to the door, and watched him kicking the stones out of his path as he went rapidly down the cliff-side. And if she had been near enough, she would have heard him muttering angrily: —

"I'm not caring! I'm not caring! The moral pride of they Binnies is ridic'lus! One would require to be a very saint to come within sight of them."

Such a wretched ending to an evening that had begun with so much hope and love! Christina stood sadly at the open door and watched her lover across the lonely sands, and felt the natural disappointment of the circumstances. Then the moon began to rise, and when she noticed this, she remembered how late her mother was away from home, and a slight uneasiness crept into her heart. She threw a plaid around her head, and was going to the neighbour's where she expected to find her, when Janet appeared.

She came up to the cliff slowly, and her face was far graver than ordinary when she entered the cottage, and with a pious ejaculation threw off her shawl.

"What kept you at all, Mother? I was just going to seek you."

"Watty Robertson has won away at last."

"When did he die?"

"He went away with the tide. He was called just at the turn. Ah, Christina, it is loving and dying all the time! Life is love and death; for what is our life? It is even a vapour that appeareth for a little time, and then vanisheth away."

"But Watty was well ready for the change, Mother?"

"He went away with a smile. And I staid by poor Lizzie, for I have drank of the same cup, and I know how bitter was the taste of it. Old

Elspeth McDonald stretched the corpse, and her and I had a change of words; but Lizzie was with me."

"What for did you clash at such a like time?"

"She covered up his face, and I said: ' Stop your hand, Elspeth. Don't you go to cover Watty's face now. He never did ill to any one while he lived, and there's no need to hide his face when he is dead.' And we had a bit stramash about it, for I can't abide to hide up the face that is honest and well loved, and Lizzie said I was right, and so Elspeth went off in a tiff."

"I think there must be 'tiffs' floating about in the air to-night. Jamie and Andrew have had a falling out, and Jamie went away far less than pleased with me."

"What's to do between them?"

"Jamie met with an old friend who was hungry and thirsty, and he went with him to the 'public' instead of going to the boat for Andrew, as he promised to do. You know how Andrew feels about a word broken."

"*Toots!* Andrew Binnie has a deal to learn yet. You should have told him it was better to show mercy, than to stick at a mouthful of words. Had you never a soft answer to throw at the two fractious fools?"

" How could I interfere? "

" Finely! If you don't know the right way to throw with a thrawn man, like Andrew, and to come round a soft man, like Jamie, I'm sorry for you! A woman with a thimble-full of woman-wit could ravel them both up — ravel them up like a cut of worsteds."

" Well, the day is near over. The clock will chap twelve in ten minutes, and I'm going to my bed. I'm feared you won't sleep much, Mother. You look awake to your instep."

" Never mind. I have some good thoughts for the sleepless. Folks don't sleep well after seeing a man with wife and bairns round him look death and judgment in the face."

" But Watty looked at them smiling, you said? "

" He did. Watty's religion went to the bottom and extremity of things. I'll be asking this night for grace to live with, and then I'll get grace to die with when my hour comes. You need n't fash your heart about me. Sleeping or waking, I am in His charge. Nor about Jamie; he'll be all right the morn. Nor about Andrew, for I'll tell him not to make a Pharisee of himself — he has his own failing, and it is n't far to seek."

And it is likely Janet had her intended talk with her son, for nothing more was said to

Jamie about his neglect of duty; and the little cloud was but a passing one, and soon blew over. Circumstances favoured oblivion. Christina's love encompassed both her brother and her lover, and Janet's womanly tact turned every shadow into sunshine, and disarmed all suspicious or doubtful words. Also, the fishing season was an unusually good one; every man was of price, and few men were better worth their price than Jamie Logan. So an air of prosperity and happiness filled each little cottage, and Andrew Binnie was certainly saving money — a condition of affairs that always made him easy to live with.

As for the women of the village, they were in the early day up to their shoulders in work, and in the more leisurely evenings, they had Christina's marriage and marriage presents to talk about. The girl had many friends and relatives far and near, and every one remembered her. It was a set of china from an aunt in Crail, or napery from some cousins in Kirkcaldy, or quilts from her father's folk in Largo, and so on, in a very charming monotony. Now and then a bit of silver came, and once a very pretty American clock. And there was not a quilt or a tablecloth, a bit of china or silver, a petticoat or a ribbon, that the whole village did not examine, and discuss, and offer their congratulations over.

Christina and her mother quite enjoyed this popular manifestation of interest, and Jamie was not at all averse to the good-natured familiarity. And though Andrew withdrew from such occasions, and appeared to be rather annoyed than pleased by the frequent intrusion of strange women, neither Janet nor Christina heeded his attitude very much.

"What for would we be caring?" queried the mother. "There is just one woman in the world to Andrew. If it was Sophy's wedding-presents now, he would be in a wonder over them! But he is not wanting you to marry at all, Christina. Men are a selfish lot. Somehow, I think he has taken a doubt or a dislike to Jamie. He thinks he is n't good enough for you."

"He is as good as I want him. I 'm feared for men as particular as Andrew. They are whiles gey ill to live with. Andrew has not had a smile for a body for a long time, and he has been making money. I wonder if there is aught wrong between Sophy and himself."

"You might away to Largo and ask after the girl. She has n't been here in a good while. And I 'm thinking yonder talk she had with you anent Archie Braelands was n't all out of her own head."

So that afternoon Christina put on her kirk

dress, and went to Largo to see Sophy. Her walk took her over a lonely stretch of country, though, as she left the coast, she came to a lovely land of meadows, with here and there waving plantations of young spruce or fir trees. Passing the entrance to one of these sheltered spots, she saw a servant driving leisurely back and forward a stylish dog-cart; and she had a sudden intuition that it belonged to Braelands. She looked keenly into the green shadows, but saw no trace of any human being; yet she had not gone far, ere she was aware of light footsteps hurrying behind her, and before she could realise the fact, Sophy called her in a breathless, fretful way "to wait a minute for her." The girl came up flushed and angry-looking, and asked Christina, "whatever brought her that far?"

"I was going to Largo to see you. Mother was getting worried about you. It's long since you were near us."

"I am glad I met you. For I was wearied with the sewing to-day, and I asked Aunt to let me have a holiday to go and see you; and now we can go home together, and she will never know the differ. You must not tell her but what I have been to Pittendurie. My goodness! It is lucky I met you."

"But where have you been, Sophy?"

" I have been with a friend, who gave me a long drive."

"Who would that be?"

" Never you mind. There is nothing wrong to it. You may trust me for that, Christina. I was fairly worn out, and Aunt has n't a morsel of pity. She thinks I ought to be glad to sew from Monday morning to Saturday night, and I tell you it hurts me, and gives me a cough, and I had to get a breath of sea-air or die for it. So a friend gave me what I wanted."

" But if you had come to our house, you could have got the sea-air finely. Sophy! Sophy! I am misdoubting what you tell me. How came you in the wood? "

" We were taking a bit walk by ourselves there. I love the smell of the pines, and the peace, and the silence. It rests me; and I did n't want folks spying, and talking, and going with tales to Aunt. She ties me up shorter than needs be now."

" He was a mean fellow to leave you here all by yourself."

" I made him do it. Goodness knows, he is fain enough to be seen by high and low with me. But Andrew would not like it; he is that jealous-natured — and I just *be* to have some rest and fresh air."

" Andrew would gladly give you both."

"Not he! He is away to the fishing, or about his business, one way or another, all the time. And I am that weary of stitch, stitch, stitching, I could cry at the thought of it."

"Was it Archie Braelands that gave you the drive?"

"Ay, it was. Archie is just my friend, nothing more. I have told him, and better told him, that I am to marry Andrew."

"He is a scoundrel then to take you out."

"He is nothing of the kind. He is just a friend. I am doing Andrew no wrong, and myself a deal of good."

"Then why are you feared for people seeing you?"

"I am not feared. But I don't want to be the wonder and the talk of every idle body. And I am not able to bear my aunt's nag, nag, nag at me. I wish I was married. It isn't right of Andrew to leave me so much to myself. It will be his own fault if he loses me altogether. I am worn out with Aunt Kilgour, and my life is a fair weariness to me."

"Andrew is getting everything brawly ready for you. I wish I could tell you what grand plans he has for your happiness. Be true to Andrew, Sophy, and you will be the happiest bride, and the best loved wife in all Scotland."

" Plans! What plans? What has he told you? "

" I am not free to speak, Sophy. I should not have said a word at all. I hope you will just forget I have."

" Indeed I will not! I will make Andrew tell me his plans. Why should he tell you, and not me? It is a shame to treat me that way, and he shall hear tell of it."

" Sophy! Sophy! I would as lief you killed me, as told Andrew I had given you a hint of his doings. He would never forgive me. I can no forgive myself. Oh what a foolish, wicked woman I have been to say a word to you! " and Christina burst into passionate weeping.

" *Whist!* Christina; I'll never tell him, not I! I know well you slipped the words to pleasure me. But giff-gaff makes us good friends, and so you must just walk to the door with me and pass a word with my aunt, and say neither this nor that about me, and I will forget you ever said Andrew had such a thing as a ' plan ' about me."

The proposal was not to Christina's mind, but she was ready to face any contingency rather than let Andrew know she had given the slightest hint of his intentions. She understood what joy he had in the thought of telling his great news to Sophy at its full time, and how angry he

55

would naturally feel at any one who interfered with his designs. In a moment, without intention, with the very kindest of motives, she had broken her word to her brother, and she was as miserable as a woman could be over the unhappy slip. And Sophy's proposal added to her remorse. It made her virtually connive at Sophy's intercourse with Archie Braelands, and she felt herself to be in a great strait. In order to favour her brother she had spoken hastily, and the swift punishment of her folly was that she must now either confess her fault or tacitly sanction a wrong against him.

For the present, she could see no way out of the difficulty. To tell Andrew would be to make him suspicious on every point. He would then doubtless find some other hiding place for his money, and if any accident did happen, her mother, and Sophy, and all Andrew loved, would suffer for her indiscretion. She took Sophy's reiterated promise, and then walked with the girl to her aunt's house. It was a neat stone dwelling, with some bonnets and caps in the front window, and when the door was opened, a bell rang, and Mistress Kilgour came hastily from an inner room. She looked pleased when she saw Sophy and Christina, and said: —

" Come in, Christina. I am glad you brought Sophy home in such good time. For I'm in a state of perfect flustration this afternoon. Here's a bride gown and bonnet to make, and a sound of more work coming."

" Who is to be married, Miss Kilgour? "

" Madame Kilrin of Silverhawes — a second affair, Christina, and she more than middle-aged."

" She is rich, though? "

" That's it! rich, but made up of odds and ends, and but one eye to see with : a prelatic woman, too, seeking all things her own way."

" And the man ? Who is he? "

" He is a lawyer. Them gentry have their fingers in every pie, hot or cold. However, I 'm wishing them nothing but good. Madame is a constant customer. Come, come, Christina, you are not going already? "

" I am hurried to-night, Mistress Kilgour. Mother is alone. Andrew is away to Greenock on business."

" So you came back with Sophy. I am glad you did. There are some folks that are o'er ready to take charge of the girl, and some that seem to think she can take charge of herself. Oh, she knows fine what I mean ! " And Miss Kilgour pointed her fore-finger at Sophy and shook her head until all the flowers in her cap and all the ringlets on her front hair dangled in unison.

Sophy had turned suddenly sulky and made no reply, and Miss Kilgour continued: "It is her way always, when she has been to your house, Christina. Whatever do you say to her? Is there anything agee between Andrew and herself? Last week and the week before, she came back from Pittendurie in a temper no saint could live with."

"I'm so miserable, Aunt. I am miserable every hour of my life."

"And you wouldn't be happy unless you were miserable, Sophy. Don't mind her talk, Christina. Young things in love don't know what they want."

"I am sick, Aunt."

"You are in love, Sophy, and that is all there is to it. Don't go, Christina. Have a cup of tea first?"

"I cannot stop any longer. Good-bye, Sophy. I'll tell Andrew to come and give you a walk to-morrow. Shall I?"

"If you like to. He will not come until Sunday, though; and then he will be troubled about walking on the Sabbath day. I'm not caring to go out."

"That is a lie, Sophy Traill!" cried her aunt. "It is the only thing you do care about."

"You had better go home, Christina," said Sophy, with a sarcastic smile, "or you will be getting a share of temper that does not belong to you. I am well used to it."

Christina made an effort to consider this remark as a joke, and under this cover took her leave. She was thankful to be alone with herself. Her thoughts and feelings were in a tumult; she could not bring any kind of reason out of their chaos. Her chagrin at her own folly was sharp and bitter. It made her cry out against herself, as she trod rapidly her homeward road. Almost inadvertently, because it was the shortest and most usual way, she took the route that led her past Braelands. The great house was thrown open, and on the lawns was a crowd of handsomely dressed men and women, drinking tea at little tables set under the trees and among the shrubbery. Christina merely glanced at the brave show of shifting colour, and passed more quickly onward, the murmur of conversation and the ripple of laughter pursuing her a little way, for the evening was warm and quiet.

She thought of Sophy among this gay crowd, and felt the incongruity of the situation, and a sense of anger sprung up in her breast at the girl's wicked impatience and unfaithfulness. It had caused her also to err, for she had been tempted by it to speak words which had been a violation of her own promise, and yet which had really done no good.

"She was always one of those girls that led others into trouble," she reflected. "Many a scolding she has got me when I was a wee thing, and to think that now! with the promise to Andrew warm on my lips, I have put myself in her power! It is too bad! It is not believable!"

She was glad when she came within sight of the sea; it was like a glimpse of home. The damp, fresh wind with its strong flavour of brine put heart into her, and the few sailors and fishers she met, with their sweethearts on their arms and their blue shirts open at their throats, had all a merry word or two to say to her. When she reached her home, she found Andrew sitting at a little table looking over some papers full of strange marks and columns of figures. His quick glance, and the quiet assurance of his love contained in it, went sorely to her heart. She would have fallen at his feet and confessed her unadvised admission to Sophy gladly, but she doubted whether it would be the kindest and wisest thing to do.

And then Janet joined them, and she had any number of questions to ask about Sophy, and Christina, to escape being pressed on this subject, began to talk with forced interest of Madame Kilrin's marriage. So, between this and that, the evening got over without suspicion, and Christina carried her miserable sense of dis-

loyalty to bed and to sleep with her — literally
to sleep, for she dreamed all night of the circumstance, and awakened in the morning with a
heart as heavy as lead.

"But it is just what I deserve!" she said
crossly to herself, as she laced her shoes; "what
need had I to be caring about Sophy Traill and
her whims? She is a dissatisfied lass at the
best, and her love affairs are beyond my sort-
ing. Serves you right, Christina Binnie! You
might know, if anybody might, that they who
put their oar into another's boat are sure to
get their fingers rapped. They deserve it too."

However, Christina could not willingly dwell
long on sorrowful subjects. She was always
inclined to subdue trouble swiftly, or else to shake
it away from her. For she lived by intuition,
rather than by reason; and intuition is born of,
and fed by, home affection and devout religion.
Something too of that insight which changes
faith into knowledge, and which is the birthright
of primitive natures, was hers; and she divined,
she knew not how, that Sophy would be true to
her promise, and not say a word which would
lead Andrew to doubt her. And so far she was
right. Sophy had many faults, but the idea of
breaking her contract with Christina did not
even occur to her.

She wondered what plans Andrew had, and

what good surprise he was preparing for her, but she was in no special hurry to find it out. The knowledge might bring affairs to a permanent crisis between her and Andrew, — might mean marriage — and Sophy dreaded to face this question, with all its isolating demands. Her "friendship" with Archie Braelands was very sweet to her; she could not endure to think of any event which must put a stop to it. She enjoyed Archie's regrets and pleadings. She liked to sigh a little and cry a little over her hard fate; to be sympathised with for it; to treat it as if she could not escape from it ; and yet to be nursing in her heart a passionate hope to do so.

And after all, the process of reflection is un-natural and uncommon to nine tenths of human-ity; and so Christina lifted her daily work and interests, and tried to forget her fault. And in-deed, as the weeks went on, she tried to believe it had been no fault, for Sophy was much kinder to Andrew for some time ; this fact being readily discernible in Andrew's cheerful moods, and in the more kindly interest which he then took in his home matters.

"For it is well with us, when it is well with Sophy Traill, and we have the home weather she lets us have," Janet often remarked. The assertion had a great deal of truth in it. Sophy, from her chair in Mistress Kilgour's workroom, greatly influenced the domestic happiness of the Binnie cottage, even though they neither saw her, nor spoke her name. But her moods made Andrew happy or miserable, and Andrew's moods made Janet and Christina happy or miserable; so sure and so wonderful a thing is human solidarity. Yes indeed! For what one of us has not known some man or woman, never seen, who holds the thread of a destiny and yet has no knowledge concerning it. This thought would make life a desperate tangle if we did not also know that One, infinite in power and mercy, guides every event to its predestined and its wisest end.

For a little while after Christina's visit, Sophy was particularly kind to Andrew; then there came a sudden change, and Christina noticed that her brother returned from Largo constantly with a heavy step and a gloomy face. Occasionally he admitted to her that he had been "sorely disappointed," but as a general thing he shut himself in his room and sulked as only men know how to sulk, till the atmosphere of the house was tingling with suppressed temper, and every one was on the edge of words that the tongue meant to be sharp as a sword.

One morning in October, Christina met her brother on the sands, and he said, " I will take the boat and give you a sail, if you like, Christina. There is only a pleasant breeze."

"I wish you would, Andrew," she answered. "This little northwester will blow every weariful thought away."

"I'm feared I have been somewhat cross and ill to do for, lately. Mother says so."

"Mother does not say far wrong. You have lost your temper often, Andrew, and consequent your common sense. And it is not like you to be unfair, not to say unkind; you have been that more than once, and to two who love you dearly."

Andrew said no more until they were on the bay, then he let the oars drift, and asked : —

"What did you think of Sophy the last time you saw her? Tell me truly, Christina."

"Who knows aught about Sophy? She hardly knows her own mind. You cannot tell what she is thinking about by her face, any more than you can tell what she is going to do by her words. She is as uncertain as the wind, and it has changed since you lifted the oars. Is there anything new to fret yourself over?"

"Ay, there is. I cannot get sight of her."

"Are you twenty-seven years old, and of such a beggary of capacity as not to be able to concert time and place to see her?"

" But if she herself is against seeing me, then how am I going to manage? "

"What way did you find out that she was against seeing you? "

" Whatever else could I think, when I get no other thing but excuses? First, she was gone away for a week's rest, and Mistress Kilgour said I had better not trouble her — she was that nervous."

" Where did she go to? "

" I don't believe she was out of her aunt's house. I am sure the postman was astonished when I told him she was away, and her aunt's face was very confused-like. Then when I went again she had a headache, and could hardly speak a word to me; and she never named about the week's holiday. And the next time there was a ball dress making; and the next she had gone to the minister's for her 'token,' and when I said I would go there and meet her, I was told not to think of such a thing; and so on, and so on, Christina. There is nothing but put-offs and put-bys, and my heart is full of sadness and fearful wonder."

" And if you do see her, what then, Andrew? "

" She is that low-spirited I do not know how to talk to her. She has little to say, and sits with her seam, and her eyes cast down, and all her pretty, merry ways are gone far away. I

5   65

wonder where! Do you think she is ill, Christina?" he asked drearily.

"No, I do not, Andrew."

"Her mother died of a consumption, when she was only a young thing, you know."

"That is no reason why Sophy should die of a consumption. Andrew, have you ever told her what your plans are? Have you told her she may be a lady and live in London if it pleases her? Have you told her that you will soon be *Captain Binnie* of the North Sea fleet?"

"No, no! What for would I bribe the girl? I want her free given love. I want her to marry plain Andrew Binnie. I will tell her everything the very hour she is my wife. That is the joy I look forward to. And it is right, is it not?"

"No. It is all wrong. It is all wrong. Girls like men that have the spirit to win siller and push their way in the world."

"I cannot thole the thought of Sophy marrying me for my money."

"You think o'er much of your money. Ask yourself whether in getting money you have got good, or only gold. And about marrying Sophy, it is not in your hand. Marriages are made in heaven, and unless there has been a booking of your two names above, I am feared

all your courting below will come to little.
Yet it is your duty to do all you can to win
the girl you want; and I can tell you what
will win Sophy Traill, if anything on earth
will win her."

Then she pointed out to him how fond Sophy
was of fine dress and delicate living; how she
loved roses, and violets, and the flowers of the
garden, so much better than the pale, salt blossoms of the sea rack, however brilliant their
colours; how she admired such a house as Braelands, and praised the glory of the peacock's
trailing feathers. "The girl is not born for a
poor man's wife," she continued, "her heart
cries out for gold, and all that gold can buy;
and if you are set on Sophy, and none but
Sophy, you will have to win her with what she
likes best, or else see some other man do so."

"Then I will be buying her, and not winning
her."

"Oh you unspeakable man! Your conceit is
just extraordinary! If you wanted any other
good thing in life, from a big ship to a gold ring,
would you not expect to buy it? Would your
loving it, and wanting it, be sufficient? Jamie
Logan knew well what he was about, when he
brought us the letter from the Hendersons' firm.
I love Jamie very dearly; but I'm free to confess the letter came into my consideration."

Talking thus, with the good wind blowing her words into his heart, Christina soon inspired Andrew with her own ideas and confidence. His face cleared; he began to row with his natural energy; and as they stepped on the wet sands together, he said almost joyfully: —

"I will take your advice, Christina. I will go and tell Sophy everything."

"Then she will smile in your face, she will put her hand in your hand; maybe, she will give you a kiss, for she will be thinking in her heart, 'how brave and how clever my Andrew is! And he will be taking me to London and making me a lady!' and such thoughts breed love, Andrew. You are well enough, and few men handsomer or better — unless it be Jamie Logan — but it isn't altogether the man; it is what the man *can do*."

"I'll go and see Sophy to-morrow."

"Why not to-day?"

"She is going to Mariton House to fit a dress and do some sewing. Her aunt told me so."

"If I was you, I would not let her sew for strangers any longer. Go and ask her to marry you at once, and do not take 'no' from her."

"Your words stir my heart to the bottom of it, and I will do as you say, Christina; for Sophy has grown into my life, like my own

68

folk, and the sea, and the stars, and my boat, and my home. And if she will love me the better for the news I have to tell her, I am that far gone in love with her I must even put wedding on that ground. Win her I must; or else die for her."

"Win her, surely; die for her, nonsense! No man worth the name of man would die because a woman would n't marry him. God has made more than one good woman, more than one fair woman."

"Only one woman for Andrew Binnie."

"To be sure, if you choose to limit yourself in that way. I think better of you. And as for dying for a woman, I don't believe in it."

"Poor Matt Ballantyne broke his heart about Jessie Graham."

"It was a very poor heart then. Nothing mends so soon as a good heart. It trusts in the Omnipotent, and gets strength for its need, and then begins to look around for good it can do, or make for others, or take to itself. If Matt broke his heart for Jessie, Jessie would have been poorly cared for by such a weak kind of a heart. She is better off with Neil McAllister, no doubt."

"You have done me good, Christina. I have not heard so many sound observes in a long time."

And with that Janet came to the cliff-top and called to them to hurry. "Step out!" she cried, "here is Jamie Logan with a pocket full of great news; and the fish is frying itself black, while you two are daundering, as if it was your very business and duty to keep hungry folk waiting their dinner for you."

CHAPTER IV

THE LASH OF THE WHIP

WITH a joyful haste Christina went forward, leaving her brother to follow in more sober fashion. Jamie came to the cliff-top to meet her, and Janet from the cottage door beamed congratulations and radiant sympathy.

" I have got my berth on the Line, Christina! I am to sail next Friday from Greenock, so I 'll start at once, my dearie! And I am the happiest lad in Fife to-day!"

He had his arms around her as he spoke, and he kissed her smiles and glad exclamations off her lips before she could put them into words. Then Andrew joined them, and after clasping hands with Jamie and Christina, he went slowly into the cottage, leaving the lovers alone outside. Janet was all excitement.

" I 'm like to greet with the good news, Andrew," she said; " it came so unexpected. Jamie was just daundering over the sands, kind of down-hearted, he said, and wondering if he would stay through the winter and fish with

71

Peddie or not, when little Maggie Johnston cried out, ' there is a big letter for you, Jamie Logan,' and he went and got it, and, lo and behold! it was from the Hendersons themselves! And they are needing Jamie now, and he'll just go at once, he says. There's luck for you! I am both laughing and crying with the pride and the pleasure of it! "

" I wouldn't make such a fuss, anyway, Mother. It is what Jamie has been looking for and ex-pecting, and I am glad he has won to it at last.'

" Fuss indeed! Plenty of ' fuss ' made over sorrow; why not over joy? And if you think me a fool for it, I'm not sure but I might call you my neighbour, if it was only Sophy Traill or her affairs to be ' fussed ' over."

" Never mind Sophy, Mother. It is Jamie and Christina now, and Christina knows her happiness is dear to me as my own."

" Well then, show it, Andrew. Show it, my lad! We must do what we can to put heart into poor Jamie; for when all is said and done, he is going to foreign parts and leaving love and home behind." And she walked to the door and looked at Jamie and Christina, who were standing on the cliff-edge together, deeply engaged in a conversation that was of the high-est interest to themselves. " I have fancied you have been a bit shy with Jamie since yon time he set an old friend before his promise to you, Andrew; but what then?"

"I wish Christina had married among our own folk. I have no wrong to say in particular of Jamie Logan, but I think my sister might have made her life with some good man a bit closer to her."

"I thought, Andrew, that you were able to look sensibly at what comes and goes. If it was a matter of business, you would be the first to see the advantage of building your dyke with the stones you could get at. And you may believe me or not, but there's a deal of the successful work of this life carried through on that principle. Well, in marrying it is just as wise. The lad you *can get*, is happen better than the lad you *want*. Anyhow Christina is going to marry Jamie; and I'm sure he is that loving and pleasant, and that fond of her, that I have no doubt she will be happy as the day is long."

"I hope it is the truth, Mother, that you are saying."

"It is; but some folks won't see the truth, though they are dashing their noses against it. None so blind as they who won't see."

"Well, it isn't within my right to speak to-day."

"Yes, it is. It is your right and place to

speak all the good and hopeful words you can think of. Don't be dour, Andrew. Man! man! how hard it is to rejoice with them that do rejoice! It takes more Christianity to do that than most folks carry around with them."

"Mother, you are a perfectly unreasonable woman. You flyte at me, as if I was a laddie of ten years old — but I 'll not dare to say but what you do me a deal of good;" and Andrew's face brightened as he looked at her.

"You would hardly do the right thing, if I didn't flyte at you, Andrew. And maybe I would n't do it myself, if I was not watching you; having nobody to scold and advise is very like trying to fly a kite without wind. Go to the door and call in Jamie and Christina. We ought to take an interest in their bit plans and schemes; and if we take it, we ought to show we take it."

Then Andrew rose and went to the open door, and as he went he laid his big hand on his mother's shoulder, and a smile flew from face to face, and in its light every little shadow vanished. And Jamie was glad to bring in his promised bride, and among her own people as they eat together, talk over the good that had come to them, and the changes that were incident to it. And thus an hour passed swiftly away, and then "farewells" full of love and hope, and laughter and tears, and hand-clasping, and good words, were said; and Jamie went off to his new life, leaving a thousand pleasant hopes and expectations behind him.

After he was fairly out of sight, and Christina stood looking tearfully into the vacancy where his image still lingered, Andrew led her to the top of the cliff, and they sat down together. It was an exquisite afternoon, full of the salt and sparkle of the sea; and for awhile both remained silent, looking down on the cottages, and the creels, and the drying nets. The whole village seemed to be out, and the sands were covered with picturesque figures in sea-boots and striped hanging caps, and with the no less picturesque companion figures in striped petticoats. Some of the latter were old women, and these wore high-crowned, unbordered caps of white linen; others were young women, and these had no covering at all on their exuberant hair; but most of them displayed long gold rings in their ears, and bright scarlet or blue kerchiefs round their necks. Andrew glanced from these figures to his sister; and touching her striped petticoat, he said: —

"You 'll be changing this for what they call a gown, when you go to Glasgow! How soon is that to be, Christina?"

"When Jamie has got well settled in his place. It would n't be prudent before."

"About the New Year, say?"

"Ay; about the New Year."

"I am thinking of giving you a silk gown for your wedding."

"O Andrew! if you would! A silk gown would set me up above every thing! I'll never forget such a favour as that."

"I'll do it."

"And Sophy will see to the making of it. Sophy has a wonderful taste about trimming, and the like of that. Sophy will stand up with me, and you will be Jamie's best man; won't you, Andrew?"

"Ay, Sophy will see to the making of it. Few can make a gown look as she can. She is a clever bit thing" — then after a pause he added sadly, "there was one thing I did not tell you this morning; but it is a circumstance I feel very badly about."

"What is it? You know well that I shall feel with you."

"It is the way folks keep hinting this and that to me; but more, that I am mistrusting Mistress Kilgour. I saw a young fellow standing at the shop door talking to her the other morning very confidential-like — a young fellow that could not have any lawful business with her."

"What kind of a person was he?"

"A large, dark man, dressed like a picture in

a tailor's window. His servant-man, in a livery of brown and yellow, was holding the horses in a fine dog-cart. I asked Jimmy Faulds what his name was, and he laughed and said it was Braelands of Braelands, and he should think I knew it; and then he looked at me that queer, that I felt as if his eyes had told me of some calamity. 'What is he doing at Mistress Kilgour's?' I asked, as soon as I could get myself together, and Jimmy answered, 'I suppose he is ordering Madame Braelands' millinery;' and then he snickered and laughed again, and I had hard lines to keep my hands from striking him."

" What for at all ? "

" I don't know. I wish I did."

" If I give you my advice, will you take it ? "

" I will."

"Then for once — if you don't want Braelands to win Sophy from you — put your lover's fears and shamefacedness behind your back. Just remember who and what you are, and what you are like to be, and go and tell Sophy everything, and ask her to marry you next Monday morning. Take gold in your pocket, and buy her a wedding gift — a ring, or a brooch, or some bonnie thing or other ; and promise her a trip to Edinburgh or London, or any other thing she fancies."

" We have not been 'cried' yet. And the

names must be read in the kirk for **three** Sundays."

"Oh man! Cannot you get a licence? It will cost you a few shillings, but what of that? You are too slow, Andrew. If you don't take care, and make haste, Braelands will run away with your wife before your very eyes."

"I'll not believe it. It could not be. The thing is unspeakable, and unbearable. I'll face my fate the morn, and I'll know the best — or the worst of what is coming to me."

"Look for good, and have good, that is, **if** you don't let the good hour go by. You, Andrew Binnie! that can manage a boat when the north wind is doing its mightiest, are you going to be one of the cony kind, when it comes to a slip of a girl like Sophy? I can not think it, for you know what Solomon said of such — 'Oh Son, it is a feeble folk.'"

"I don't come of feeble folk, body nor soul; and as I have said, I will have the whole matter out with Sophy to-morrow."

"Good — but better *do* than say."

The next morning a swift look of intelligence passed between Andrew and Christina at breakfast, and about eleven o'clock Andrew said, "I'll away now to Largo, and settle the business we were speaking of, Christina." She looked up at him critically, and thought she had never

78

seen a handsomer man. Though only a fisherman, he was too much a force of nature to be
vulgar. He was the incarnation of the grey, old
village, and of the North Sea, and of its stormy
winds and waters. Standing in his boots he was
over six feet, full of pluck and fibre, a man
not made for the town and its narrow doorways,
but for the great spaces of the tossing ocean.
His face was strong and finely formed; his eyes
grey and open — as eyes might be that had
so often searched the thickest of the storm
with unquailing glance. A sensitive flush over-
spread his brow and cheeks as Christina gazed
at him, and he said nervously : —

"I will require to put on my best clothes;
won't I, Christina?"

She laid her hand on his arm, and shook her
head with a pleasant smile. She was regarding
with pride and satisfaction her brother's fine
figure, admirably shown in the elastic grace of
his blue Guernsey. She turned the collar low
enough to leave his round throat a little bare,
and put his blue flannel *Tam o' Shanter* over
his close, clustering curls. "Go as you are,"
she said. "In that dress you feel at home, and
at ease, and you look ten times the man you
do in your broadcloth. And if Sophy cannot
like her fisher-lad in his fisher-dress, she is n't
worthy of him."

He was much pleased with this advice, for it precisely sorted with his own feelings; and he stooped and kissed Christina, and she sent him away with a smile and a good wish. Then she went to her mother, who was in a little shed salting some fish. "Mother," she cried, "Andrew has gone to Largo."

"Like enough. It would be stranger, if he had stopped at home."

"He has gone to ask Sophy to marry him next week — next Monday."

"Perfect nonsense! We'll have no such marrying in a hurry, and a corner. It will take a full month to marry Andrew Binnie. What would all our folks say, far and near, if they were not bid to the wedding? Set to that, you have to be married first. Marrying isn't like Christmas, coming every year of our Lord; and we *be* to make the most of it. I'll not give my consent to any such like hasty work. Why, they are not even 'called' in the kirk yet."

"Andrew can get a licence."

"Andrew can get a fiddle-stick! None of the Binnies were ever married, but by word of the kirk, and none of them shall be, if I can help it. Licence indeed! Buying the right to marry for a few shillings, and the next thing will be a few more shillings for the right to unmarry. I'll not hear tell of such a way."

" But, Mother, if Andrew does not get Sophy at once, he may lose her altogether."

" *Humph !* No great loss."

" The biggest loss in the world that Andrew can have. Things are come to a pass. If Andrew does not marry her at once, I am feared Braelands will carry her off."

" He is welcome to her."

" No, no, Mother! Do you want Braelands to get the best of Andrew?"

" The like of him get the best of Andrew! I'll not believe it. Sophy is n't beyond all sense of right and feeling. If, after all these years, she left Andrew for that fine gentleman, she would be a very Jael of deceit and treachery. I wish I had told her about her mother's second cousin, bonnie Lizzie Lauder."

" What of her? I never heard tell, did I, Mother?"

" No. We don't speak of Lizzie now."

" Why then?"

" She was very bonnie, and she was very like Sophy about hating to work; and she was never done crying to all the gates of pleasure to open wide and let her enter. And she went in."

" Well, Mother? Is that all?"

" No. I wish in God's mercy it was! The avenging gates closed on her. She is shut up in hell. There, I'll say no more."

6   81

" Yes, Mother. You will ask God's mercy for her. It never faileth."

Janet turned away, and lifted her apron to her eyes, and stood so silent for a few minutes. And Christina left her alone, and went back into the house place, and began to wash up the breakfast-cups and cut up some vegetables for their early dinner. And by-and-by her mother joined her, and Christina began to tell how Andrew had promised her a silk gown for her wedding. This bit of news was so wonderful and delightful to Janet, that it drove all other thoughts far from her. She sat down to discuss it with all the care and importance the subject demanded. Every colour was considered; and when the colour had been decided, there was then the number of yards and the kind of trimming to be discussed, and the manner of its making, and the person most suitable to undertake the momentous task. For Janet was at that hour angry with Mistress Kilgour, and not inclined to " put a bawbee her way," seeing that it was most likely she had been favouring Bracland's suit, and therefore a bitter enemy to Andrew.

After the noon meal, Janet took her knitting, and went to tell as many of her neighbours as it was possible to see during the short afternoon, about the silk gown her Christina was to be married in; and Christina spread her ironing table, and began to damp, and fold, and smooth the clean linen. And as she did so, she sang a verse or two of " Hunting Tower," and then she thought awhile, and then she sang again. And she was so happy, that her form swayed to her movements; it seemed to smile as she walked backwards and forwards with the finished garments or the hot iron in her hands. She was thinking of the happy home she would make for Jamie, and of all the bliss that was coming to her. For before a bird flies you may see its wings; and Christina was already pluming hers for a flight into that world which in her very ignorance she invested with a thousand unreal charms.

She did not expect Andrew back until the evening. He would most likely have a long talk with Sophy; there was so much to tell her; and when it was over, it would be in a large measure to tell again to Mistress Kilgour. Then it was likely Andrew would take tea with his promised wife, and perhaps they might have a walk afterwards; so, calculating all these things, Christina came to the conclusion that it would be well on to bed time, before she knew what arrangements Andrew had made for his marriage and his life after it.

Not a single unpleasant doubt troubled her mind; she thought she knew Sophy's nature so well; and she could hardly conceive it possible,

that the girl should have any reluctances about
a lad so well known, so good, and so handsome,
and with such a fine future before him, as Andrew Binnie. All Sophy's flights and fancies,
all her favours to young Braclands, Christina
put down to the dissatisfaction Sophy so often
expressed with her position, and the vanity
which arose naturally from her recognised
beauty and youthful grace. But to be "a settled woman," with a loving husband and "a
house of her own," seemed to Christina an irresistible offer; and she smiled to herself when
she thought of Sophy's surprise, and of the
many pretty little airs and conceits the state of
bridehood would be sure to bring forth in her
self-indulgent nature.

"She will be provoking enough, no doubt,"
she whispered as she set the iron sharply
down; "but I'll never notice it. She is very
little more than a bairn, and but a canary-headed
creature added to that. In a year or two,
Andrew, and marriage, and maybe motherhood,
will sober and settle her. And Andrew loves
her so. Most as well as Jamie loves me. For
Andrew's sake, then, I'll bear with all her provoking ways and words. She'll be *our own*,
anyway, and we be to have patience with they
of our own household. Bonnie wee Sophy."

It was about mid-afternoon when she came

to this train of forbearing and conciliating reflections. She was quite happy in it; for Christina was one of those wise women, who do not
'look into their ideals and hopes too closely.
Her face reflecting them was beautiful and
benign; and her shoulders, and hands, her sup-
ple waist and limbs, continued the symphonies
of her soft, deep, loving eyes and her smiling
mouth. Every now and then she burst into
song; and then her thrilling voice, so sweet and
fresh, had tones in it that only birds and good
women full of love may compass. Mostly the
song was a lilt or a verse which spoke for her
own heart and love; but just as the clock struck
three, she broke into a low laugh which ended
in a merry, mocking melody, and which was
evidently the conclusion of her argument concerning Sophy's behaviour as Andrew's wife —

"Toot! toot! quoth the grey-headed father,
   She 's less of a bride than a bairn;
  She 's ta'en like a colt from the heather,
   With sense and discretion to learn.

"Half-husband I trow, and half daddy,
   As humour inconstantly leans;
  The man must be patient and steady,
   That weds with a lass in her teens."

She had hardly finished the verse, when she
heard a step blending with its echoes. Her

ears rung inward; her eyes dilated with an unhappy expectancy; she put down her iron
with a sudden faint feeling, and turned her face
to the door.

Andrew entered the cottage. He looked at
her despairingly, and sinking into his chair, he
covered his wretched face with his hands.

It was not the same man who had left her a
few hours before. A change, like that which a
hot iron would make upon a green leaf, had
been made in her handsome, hopeful, happy
brother. She could not avoid an exclamation
that was a cry of terror; and she went to him
and kissed him, and murmured, she knew not
what words of pity and love. Under their influence, the flood gates of sorrow were unloosed;
he began to weep, to sob, to shake and tremble,
like a reed in a tempest.

Christina saw that his soul was tossed from
top to bottom, and in the madness of the storm,
she knew it was folly to ask " why ? " But she
went to the door, closed it, slipped forward the
bolt, and then came back to his side, waiting
there patiently until the first paroxysm of his
grief was over. Then she said softly: —

" Andrew! My brother Andrew! What sorrow has come to you? Tell Christina."

" Sophy is dead — dead and gone for me.
Oh Sophy, Sophy, Sophy ! "

86

" Andrew, tell me a straight tale. You are not a woman to let any sorrow get the mastery over you."

"Sophy has gone from me. She has played me false — and after all these years, deceived and left me."

" Then there is still the Faithful One. His love is from everlasting, to everlasting. He changeth not."

" Ay; I know," he said drearily. But he straightened himself and unfastened the button at his throat, and stood up on his feet, planting them far apart, as if he felt the earth like the reeling deck of a ship. And Christina opened the little window, and drew his chair near it, and let the fresh breeze blow upon him; and her heart throbbed hotly with anger and pity.

" Sit down in the sea wind, Andrew," she said. " There 's strength and a breath of comfort in it; and try and give your trouble words. Did you see Sophy? "

" Ay; I saw her."

" At her aunt's house? "

" No. I met her on the road. She was in a dog-cart; and the master of Braelands was driving her. I saw her, ere she saw me; and she was looking in his face as she never looked in my face. She loves him, Christina, as she never loved me."

"Did you speak to her?"

"I was that foolish, and left to myself. She was going to pass me, without a look or a word; but I could not thole the scorn and pain of it, and I called out to her, '*Sophy! Sophy!*'"

"And she did not answer you?"

"She cruddled closer to Braelands. And then he lifted the whip to hurry the horse; and before I knew what I was doing, I had the beast by the head — and the lash of the whip — struck me clean across the cheek bone."

"Oh Andrew! Andrew!" And she bent forward and looked at the outraged cheek, and murmuring, "I see the mark of it! I see the mark of it!" she kissed the long, white welt, and wetted it with her indignant tears.

Andrew sat passive under her sympathy until she asked, "Did Braelands say anything when he struck you? Had he no word of excuse?"

"He said: 'It is your own fault, fisherman. The lash was meant for the horse, and not for you.'"

"Well?"

"And I was in a passion; and I shouted some words I should not have said — words I never said in my life before. I did n't think the like of them were in my heart."

"I don't blame you, Andrew."

" I blame myself though. Then I bid Sophy get out of the cart and come to me; — and — "

" Yes, dear ? "

" And she never moved or spoke; she just covered her face with her hands, and gave a little scream; — for no doubt I had frighted her — and Braelands, he got into the de'il's own rage then, and dared me to call the lady ' Sophy ' again; ' for,' said he, ' she will be my wife before many days'; and with that, he struck the horse savagely again and again, and the poor beast broke from my hand, and bounded for'ard; and I fell on my back, and the wheels of the cart grazed the soles of my shoon as they passed me."

" And then? "

" I don't know how long I lay there."

" And they went on and left you lying in the highway? "

" They went on."

" The wicked lass! Oh the wicked, heartless lass ! "

" You are not able to judge her, Christina.'

" But you can judge Braelands. Get a warrant for the scoundrel the morn. He is without the law."

" Then I would make Sophy the common talk, far and near. How could I wrong Sophy to right myself? "

" But the whip lash! the whip lash! Andrew. You cannot thole the like of that! "

" There was One tholed for me the lash and the buffet, and answer'd never a word. I can thole the lash for Sophy's sake. A poor love I would have for Sophy, if I put my own pride before her good name. If I get help 'from beyond,' I can thole the lash, Christina."

He was white through all the tan of wind, and sea, and sun; and the sweat of his suffering stood in great beads on his pallid face and brow. Christina lifted a towel, which she had just ironed, and wiped it away ; and he said feebly : —

" Thank you, dear lass ! I will go to my bed a wee."

So Christina opened the door of his room and he tottered in, swaying like a drunken man, and threw himself upon his bed. Five minutes afterward she stepped softly to his side. He was sunk in deep sleep, fathoms below the tide of grief whose waves and billows had gone over him.

" Thanks be to the Merciful ! " she whispered. " When the sorrow is too great, then He giveth His beloved sleep."

CHAPTER V

THE LOST BRIDE

THIS unforeseen and unhappy meeting forced a climax in Sophy's love affairs, which she had hitherto not dared to face. In fact, circumstances tending that way had arisen about a week previously; and it was in consequence of them, that she was publicly riding with Braelands when Andrew met them. For a long time she had insisted on secrecy in her intercourse with her "friend." She was afraid of Andrew; she was afraid of her aunt; she was afraid of being made a talk and a speculation to the gossips of the little town. And though Miss Kilgour had begun to suspect somewhat, she was not inclined to verify her suspicions. Madame Braelands was a good customer, therefore she did not wish to know anything about a matter which she was sure would be a great annoyance to that lady.

But Madame herself forced the knowledge on her. Some friend had called at Braelands and thought it right to let her know what a dangerous affair her son was engaged in. " For the girl is beautiful," she said, " there is no denying that; and she comes of fisher-folk, who have simply no idea but that love-words and love-kisses must lead to marrying and housekeeping, and who will bitterly resent and avenge a wrong done to any woman of their class, as you well know, Madame."

Madame did know this very well; and apart from her terror of a *mésalliance* for the heir of Braelands, there was the fact that his family had always had great political influence, and looked to a public recognition of it. The fisher vote was an important factor in the return of any aspirant for Parliamentary honour; and she felt keenly that Archie was endangering his whole future career by his attentions to a girl whom it was impossible he should marry, but who would have the power to arouse against him a bitter antagonism, if he did not marry her.

She affected to her friend a total indifference to the subject of her son's amusements, and she said "she was moreover sure that Archibald Braelands would never do anything to prejudice his own honour, or the honour of the humblest fisher-girl in Fifeshire." But all the same, her heart was sick with fear and anxiety; and as soon as her informant had gone, she ordered her carriage, dressed herself in all her braveries, and drove hastily to Mistress Kilgour's.

At that very hour, this lady was fussing and fuming angrily at her niece. Sophy had insisted on going for a walk, and in the altercation attending this resolve, Mistress Kilgour had unadvisably given speech to her suspicions about Sophy's companion in these frequent walks, and threatened her with a revelation of these doubts to Andrew Binnie. But in spite of all, Sophy had left the house; and her aunt was nursing her wrath against her when Madame Braeland's carriage clattered up to her shop door.

Now if Madame had been a prudent woman, and kept the rein on her prideful temper, she would have found Mistress Kilgour in the very mood suitable for an ally. But Madame had also been nursing her wrath, and as soon as Mistress Kilgour had appeared, she asked angrily : —

" Where is that niece of yours, Mistress Kilgour? I should very much like to know."

The tone of the question irritated the dressmaker, and instantly her sympathies flew toward her own kith, and kin, and class. Also, her caution was at once aroused, and she answered the question, Scotch-wise, by another question : —

'What for are you requiring to see Sophy, Madame?"

" Is she in the house?"

"Shall I go and see?"

"Go and see, indeed! You know well she is not. You know she is away somewhere, walking or driving with my son — with the heir of Braelands. Oh, I have heard all about their shameful carryings-on."

"You 'll not need to use the word 'shameful' with regard to my niece, Sophy Traill, Madame Braelands. She has never earned such a like word, and she never will. You may take my say-so for that."

"It is not anybody's say-so in this case. See-ing is believing, and they have been seen to-gether, walking in Fernie wood, and down among the rocks on the Elie coast, and in many other places."

"Well and good, Madame. What by that? Young things will be young things."

"What by that? Do you, a woman of your age, ask me such a question. When a gentle-man of good blood and family, as well as great wealth, goes walking and driving with a poor girl of no family at all, do you ask what by that? Nothing but disgrace and trouble can be looked for."

"Speak for your own kin and side, Madame. And I should think a woman of your age — being at least twenty years older than myself — would know that true love never asks for a girl's pedigree. And as for 'disgrace,' Sophy Traill will never call anything like 'disgrace' to herself. I will allow that Sophy is poor, but as for family, the Traills are of the best Norse strain. They were sea-fighters, hundreds of years before they were sea-fishers; and they had been 'at home' on the North Sea, and in all the lands about it, centuries before the like of the Braelands were thought or heard tell of."

Mistress Kilgour was rapidly becoming angry, and Madame would have been wise to have noted the circumstance; but she herself was now past all prudence, and with an air of contempt she took out her jewelled watch, and beginning to slowly wind it, said : —

"My good woman, Sophy's father was a common fisherman. We have no call to go back to the time when her people were pirates and sea-robbers."

"I am *my own* woman, Madame. And I will take my oath I am not *your* woman, anyhow. And 'common' or uncommon, the fishermen of Fife call no man master but the Lord God Almighty, from whose hands they take their food, summer and winter. And I will make free to say, moreover, that if Braelands loves Sophy Traill and she loves him, worse might befall him than Sophy for a wife. For if God thinks fit to mate them, it is not Griselda Kilgour that will take upon herself to contradict the Will of Heaven."

"Don't talk rubbish, Mistress Kilgour. People who live in society have to regard what society thinks and says."

"It is no ways obligatory, Madame; the voice of God and Nature has more weight, I'm thinking, and if God links two together, you will find it gey and hard to separate them."

"I heard the girl was promised since her babyhood to a fisherman called Andrew Binnie."

"For once you have heard the truth, Madame. But you know yourself that babyhood and womanhood are two different things; and the woman has just set at naught the baby. That is all."

"No, it is not all. This Andrew Binnie is a man of great influence among the fishers, and my son cannot afford to make enemies among that class. It will be highly prejudicial to him."

"I cannot help that, Madame. Braelands is well able to row his own boat. At any rate, I am not called to take an oar in it."

"Yes, you are. I have been a good customer to you, Mistress Kilgour."

"I am not denying it; at the same time I have been a good dress and bonnet maker to you, and earned every penny-bit you have paid me. The obligation is mutual, I'm thinking."

96

"I can be a still better customer if you will prevent this gentle-shepherding and love-making. I would not even scruple at a twenty pound note, or perhaps two of them."

"*Straa!* If you were Queen of England, Madame, I would call you an insolent dastard, to try and bribe me against my own flesh and blood. You are a very Judas, to think of such a thing. Good blood! fine family! indeed! If your son is like yourself, I'm not caring for him coming into my family at all."

"Mistress Kilgour, you may close my account with you. I shall employ you no more."

"Pay me the sixteen pounds odd you owe me, and then I will shut my books forever against Braelands. Accounts are not closed till outstanding money is paid in."

"I shall send the money."

"The sight of the money would be better than the promise of it, Madame; for some of it is owing more than a twelvemonth;" and Mistress Kilgour hastily turned over to the Braelands page of her ledger, while Madame, with an air of affront and indignation, hastily left the shop.

Following this wordy battle with her dressmaker, Madame had an equally stubborn one with her son, the immediate consequence of which was that very interview whose close was

witnessed by Andrew Binnie. In this confer-
ence Braelands acknowledged his devotion to
Sophy, and earnestly pleaded for Mistress Kilgour's favour for his suit. She was now quite
inclined to favour him. Her own niece, as mistress of Braelands, would be not only a great
social success, but also a great financial one.
Madame Braelands's capacity for bonnets was
two every year; Sophy's capacity was unlim-
ited. Madame considered four dresses annually
quite extravagant; Sophy's ideas on the same
subject were constantly enlarging. And then
there would be the satisfaction of overcoming
Madame. So she yielded easily and gracefully
to Archie Braelands's petition, and thus Sophy
suddenly found herself able to do openly what
she had hitherto done secretly, and the question
of her marriage with Braelands accepted as an
understood conclusion.

At this sudden culmination of her hardly
acknowledged desires, the girl was for a short
time distracted. She felt that Andrew must
now be definitely resigned, and a strangely sad
feeling of pity and reluctance assailed her.
There were moments she knew not which lover
was dearest to her. The habit of loving Andrew
had grown through long years in her heart;
she trusted him as she trusted no other mortal ;
she was not prepared to give up absolutely all

rights in a heart so purely and so devotedly her
own. For if she knew anything, she knew right
well that no other man would ever give her the
same unfaltering, unselfish affection.

And when she dared to consider truthfully
her estimate of Archie Braelands, she judged
his love, passionate as it was, did not ring true
through all its depths. There were times when
her little *gaucheries* fretted him; when her dress
did not suit him; when he put aside an engagement with her for a sail with a lord, or a dinner
party with friends, or a social function at his
own home. Andrew put no one before her;
and even the business that kept him from her
side was all for her future happiness. Every object and every aim of his life had reference to her.
It was hard to give up such a perfect love, and
she felt that she could not see Andrew face to
face and do it. Hence her refusals to meet him,
and her shyness and silence when a meeting was
unavoidable. Hence, also, came a very peculiar ,
attitude of Andrew's friends and mates; for they
could not conceive how Andrew's implicit faith
in his love should prevent him from finding out
what was so evident to every man and woman
in Largo.

Alas! the knowledge had now come to him.
That it could have come in any harder way,
it is difficult to believe. There was only one

palliation to its misery — it was quite unpre-
meditated — but even this mitigation of the
affront hardly brought him any comfort as yet.
Braelands was certainly deeply grieved at the
miserable outcome of the meeting. He knew
the pride of the fisher race, and he had himself
a manly instinct, strong enough to understand
the undeserved humiliation of Andrew's position.
Honestly, as a gentleman, he was sorry the quarrel had taken place; as a lover, he was anxious
to turn it to his own advantage. For he saw
that, in spite of all her coldness and apparent
apathy, Sophy was affected and wounded by
Andrew's bitter imploration and its wretched
and sorrowful ending, If the man should gain
her ear and sympathy, Braelands feared for the
result. He therefore urged her to an immediate
marriage; and when Mistress Kilgour was taken
into counsel, she encouraged the idea, because
of the talk which was sure to follow such a
flagrant breach of the courtesies of life.

But even at this juncture, Sophy's vanity must
have its showing; and she refused to marry,
until at least two or three suitable dresses should
have been prepared ; so the uttermost favour that
could be obtained from the stubborn little
bride was a date somewhere within two weeks
away.

During these two weeks there was an unspeakable unhappiness in the Binnie household. For oh, how dreary are those wastes of life, left by the loved who have deserted us! These are the vacant places we water with our bitterest tears. Had Sophy died, Andrew would have said, "It is the Lord; let him do what seemeth right in his sight." But the manner and the means of his loss filled him with a dumb sorrow and rage; for in spite of his mother's and sister's urging, he would do nothing to right his own self-respect at the price of giving Sophy the slightest trouble or notoriety. Suffer! Yes, he suffered at home, where Janet and Christina continually reminded him of the insult he ought to avenge; and he suffered also abroad, where his mates looked at him with eyes full of surprise and angry inquiries.

But though the village was ringing with gossip about Sophy and young Braelands, never a man or woman in it ventured to openly question the stern, sullen, irritable man who had been so long recognised as her accepted lover. And whether he was in the boats or out of them, no one dared to speak Sophy's name in his presence. Indeed, upon the whole, he was during these days what Janet Binnie called "an ill man to live with — a man out of his senses, and falling away from his meat and his clothes."

This misery continued for about two weeks

without any abatement, and Janet's and Christina's sympathy was beginning to be tinged with resentment. It seems so unnatural and unjust, that a girl who had already done them so much wrong, and who was so far outside their daily life, should have the power to still darken their home, and infuse a bitter drop into their peculiar joys and hopes.

"I am glad the wicked lass is n't near by me," said Janet one morning, when Andrew had declared himself unable to eat his breakfast, and gone out of the cottage to escape his mother's pleadings and reproofs. "I 'm glad she is n't near me. If she was here, I could not keep my tongue from her. She should hear the truth for once, if she never heard it again. They should be words as sharp as the birch rod she ought to have had, when she first began her nonsense, and her airs and graces."

"She is a bad girl; but we must remember that she was left much to herself — no mother to guide her, no sister or brother either."

"It would have been a pity if there had been more of them. One scone of that baking is enough. The way she has treated our Andrew is abominable. Flesh and blood can't bear such doings."

As Janet made this assertion, a cousin of Sophy's came into the cottage, and answered her. "I know you are talking of Sophy," she said, "and I am not wondering at the terrivee you are making. As for me, though she is my cousin, I'll never exchange the Queen's language with her again as long as I live in this world. But all bad things come to an end, as well as good ones, and I am bringing what will put a stop at last to all this clishmaclaver about that wearisome lassie," — and with these words she handed Janet two shining white cards, tied together with a bit of silver wire.

They were Sophy's wedding cards; and she had also sent from Edinburgh a newspaper containing a notice of her marriage to Archibald Braelands. The news was very satisfactory to Janet. She held the bits of cardboard with her fingertips, looking grimly at the names upon them. Then she laughed, not very pleasantly, at the difference in the size of the cards. "He has the wee card now," she said, "and Sophy the big one; but I'm thinking the wee one will grow big, and the big one grow little before long. I will take them to Andrew myself; the sight of them will be a bitter medicine, but it will do him good. Folks may count it great gain when they get rid of a false hope."

Andrew was walking moodily about the bit of bare turf in front of the cottage door, stopping now and then to look over the sea, where the brown sails of some of the fishing boats still caught the lazy south wind. He was thinking that the sea was cloudy, and that there was an evil-looking sky to the eastward ; and then, as his mind took in at the same moment the dangers to the fishers who people the grey waters and his own sorrowful wrong, he turned and began to walk about muttering — " Lord help us ! We must bear what is sent."

Then Janet called him, and he watched for her approach. She put the cards into his hand saying, " Sophy's cousin, Isobel Murray, brought them." Her voice was full of resentment; and Andrew, not at the moment realising a custom so unfamiliar in a fishing-village, looked wonderingly in his mother's face, and then at the fateful white messengers.

" Read the names on them, Andrew man, and you 'll know then why they are sent to Pittendurie."

Then he looked steadily at the inscription, and the struggle of the inner man shook the outward man visibly. It was like a shot in the backbone. But it was only for a moment he staggered ; though he had few resources, his faith in the Cross and his confidence in himself made him a match for his hard fate. It is in such critical moments the soul reveals if it be selfish or generous, and Andrew, with a quick upward fling of the head, regained absolutely that self-control, which he had voluntarily abdicated.

"You will tell Isobel," he said, "that I wish Mistress Braelands every good thing, both for this life and the next." Then he stepped closer to his mother and kissed her; and Janet was so touched and amazed that she could not speak. But the look of loving wonder on her face was far better than words. And as she stood looking at him, Andrew put the cards in his pocket, and went down to the sea; and Janet returned to the cottage and gave Isobel the message he had sent.

But this information, so scanty and yet so conclusive, by no means satisfied the curiosity of the women. A great deal of indignation was expressed by Sophy's kindred and friends in the village at her total ignoring of their claims. They did not expect to be invited to a house like Braelands; but they did think Sophy ought to have visited them and told them all about her preparations and future plans. They were her own flesh and blood, and they deeply resented her non-recognition of the claims of kindred. Isobel, as the central figure of this dissatisfaction, was a very important person. She at least had received "cards," and the rest of the cousins to the sixth degree felt that they had been grossly slighted in the omission. So

Isobel, for the sake of her own popularity, was compelled to make common cause, and to assert positively that " she thought little of the compliment. Sophy only wanted her folk to know she was now Mistress Braelands; and she had picked her out to carry the news — good or bad news, none yet could say."

Janet was not inclined to discuss the matter with her. She was so cold about it, that Isobel quickly discovered she had " work to finish at her own house; " for she recollected that if the Binnies were not inclined to talk over the affair, there were plenty of wives and maids in Pittendurie who were eager to do so. So Janet and Christina were quickly left to their own opinions on the marriage, the first of which was, that " Sophy had behaved very badly to them."

" But I wasn't going to say bad words for Isobel to clash round the village," said Janet, " and I am gey glad Andrew took the news so man-like and so Christian-like. They can't make any speculations about Andrew now ; and that will be a sore disappointment to the hussies, for some of them are but ill-willy creatures."

" I am glad Andrew kept a brave heart, and could bring good words out of it."

" What else would you expect from Andrew ? Do you think Andrew Binnie will fret himself

one moment about a wife that is not his wife?
He would not give the de'il such a laugh over
him. You may take my word, that he will
break no commandment for any lass; and Sophy
Braelands will now have to vacate his very
thoughts."

"I am glad she is married then. If her marriage cures Andrew of that never-ending fret
about her, it will be a comfort."

"It is a cure, sure as death, as far as your
brother is concerned. Fancy Andrew Binnie
pining and worrying about Archie Braelands's
wife! The thing would be sinful, and therefore
fairly impossible to him! I'm as glad as you
are that no worse than marriage has come to
the lass; she is done with now, and I am
wishing her no more ill than she has called to
herself."

"She has brought sorrow enough to our
house," said Christina. "All the days of my
own courting have been saddened and darkened
with the worry and the care of her. Andrew
was always either that set up or that knocked
down about her, that he could not give a
thought to Jamie's and my affairs. It was only
when you talked about Sophy, or his wedding
with Sophy, that he looked as if the world was
worth living in. He was fast growing into a
real selfish man."

"*Toots*! Every one in love — men or women — are as selfish as they can be. The whole round world only holds two folk: their own self, and another. I would like to have a bit of chat before long, that did not set itself to love-making and marrying."

"Goodness, Mother! You have not chatted much with me lately about love-making and marrying. Andrew's trouble has filled the house, and you have hardly said a word about poor Jamie, who never gave either of us a heartache. I wonder where he is to-day!"

Janet thought a moment and then answered: "He would leave New York for Scotland, last Saturday. 'Tis Wednesday morning now, and he will maybe reach Glasgow next Tuesday. Then it will not take him many hours to find himself in Pittendurie."

"I doubt it. He will not be let come and go as he wants to. It would not be reasonable. He will have to obey orders. And when he gets off, it will be a kind of favour. A steamboat and a fishing-boat are two different things, Mother; forbye, Jamie is but a new hand, and will have his way to win."

"What are you talking about, you silly, fearful lassie? It would be a poor-like, heartless captain, that had not a fellow-feeling for a lad in love. Jamie will just have to tell him about yourself, and he will send the lad off with a laugh, or maybe a charge not to forget the ship's sailing-day. Hope well, and have well, lassie."

"You'll be far mistaken, Mother. I am not expecting Jamie for more than two or three trips — but he'll be thinking of me, and I can not help thinking of him."

"Think away, Christina. Loving thoughts keep out others, not as good. I wonder how it would do to walk as far as Largo, and find out all about the marriage from Griselda Kilgour. Then I would have the essentials, and something worth telling and talking about."

"I would go, Mother. Griselda will be thirsty to tell all she knows, and just distracted with the glory of her niece. She will hold herself very high, no doubt."

"Griselda and her niece are two born fools, and I am not to be put to the wall by the like of them. And it is not beyond hoping, that I'll be able to give the woman a mouthful of sound advice. She's a set-up body, but I shall disapprove of all she says."

"You may disapprove till you are black in the face, Mother, but Griselda will hold her own; she is neither flightersome, nor easy frightened. I'm feared it is going to rain. I see the glass has fallen."

"I'm not minding the 'glass.' The sky is clear, and I think far more of the sky, and the look of it, than I do of the 'glass.' I wonder at Andrew hanging it in our house; it is just sinful and unlucky to be taking the change of the weather out of His hands. But rain or fine, I am going to Largo."

As she spoke, she was taking out of her kist a fine Paisley shawl and a bonnet, and with Christina's help she was soon dressed to her own satisfaction. Fortunately one of the fishers was going with his cart to Largo, so she got a lift over the road, and reached Griselda Kilgour's early in the afternoon. There were no bonnets and caps in the window of the shop, and when Janet entered, the place had a covered-up, Sabbath-day look that kindled her curiosity. The ringing of the bell quickly brought Mistress Kilgour forward, and she also had an unusual look. But she seemed pleased to see Janet, and very heartily asked her into the little parlour behind.

"I'm just home," she said, "and I'm making myself a cup of tea ere I sort up the shop and get to my day's work again. Sit down, Janet, and take off your things, and have a cup with me. Strange days and strange doings in them lately!"

"You may well lift up your eyes and your

hands, Griselda. I never heard tell of the like. The whole village is in a flustration; and I just came o'er-by, to find out from you the long and the short of everything. I 'm feared you have been sorely put about with the wilful lass."

" Mistress Braelands had no one to lippen to but me. I had everything to look after. The Master of Braelands was that far gone in love, he was n't to be trusted with anything. But my niece has done a good job for herself."

" It is well *some one* has got good out of her treachery. She brought sorrow enough to my house. But I 'm glad it is all over, and that Braelands has got her. She would n't have suited my son at all, Griselda."

" Not in the least," answered the dressmaker with an air of offence. " How many lumps of sugar, Janet? "

" I 'm not taking sugar. Where was the lass married? "

" In Edinburgh. We did n't want any talk and fuss about the wedding, and Braelands he said to me, ' Mistress Kilgour, if you will take a little holiday, and go with Sophy to Edinburgh, and give her your help about the things she requires, we shall both of us be your life-long debtors.' And I thought Edinburgh was the proper place, and so I went with Sophy — putting up a notice on the shop door that I had gone to look at the winter fashions, and would be back to-day — and here I am, for I like to keep my word."

"You did n't keep it with my Andrew; for you promised to help him with Sophy, you promised that more than once or twice."

"No one can help a man who fights against himself, and Andrew never did prize Sophy as Braelands did; the way that man ran after the lass, and coaxed, and courted, and pleaded with her! And the bonnie things he gave her! And the stone blind infatuation of the creature! Well, I never saw the like. He was that far gone in love, there was nothing for him but standing up before the minister."

"What minister?"

"Dr. Beith of St. Andrews. Braelands sits in St. Andrews, when he is in Edinburgh for the winter season, and Dr. Beith is knowing him well. I wish you could have seen the dresses and the mantillas, the bonnets and the fineries of every sort I had to buy Sophy, not to speak of the rings and gold chains and bracelets and such things, that Braelands just laid down at her feet."

"What kind of dresses?"

"Silks and satins — white for the wedding-dress — and pink, and blue, and tartan, and what not! I tell you McFinlay and Co. were kept busy day and night for Sophy Braelands."

Then Mistress Kilgour entered into a minute description of all Sophy's beautiful things, and Janet listened attentively, not only for her own gratification, but also for that of every woman in Pittenduric. Indeed she appeared so interested that her entertainer never suspected the anger she was restraining with difficulty until her curiosity had been satisfied. But when every point had been gone over, when the last thing about Sophy's dress and appearance had been told and discussed, Janet suddenly inquired, "Have they come back to Largo yet?"

"Indeed nothing so common," answered Griselda, proudly. "They have gone to foreign lands — to France, and Italy, and Germany," — and then with a daring imagination she added, "and it's like they won't stop short of Asia and America."

"Well, Jamie Logan, my Christina's promised man is on the American line. I dare say he will be seeing her on his ship, and no doubt he will do all he can to pleasure her."

"Jamie Logan! Sophy would not think of noticing him now. It would not be proper."

"What for not? He is as good a man as Archie Braelands, and if all reports be true, a good deal better."

"*Archie* indeed! I'm thinking 'Master Braelands' would be more as it should be."

8   113

"I'll never 'master' him. He is no 'master' of mine. What for does he have a Christian name, if he is not to be called by it?"

"Well, Janet, you need not show your temper. Goodness knows, it is as short as a cat's hair. And Braelands is beyond your tongue, anyhow."

"I'm not giving him a word. Sophy will pay every debt he is owing me and mine. The lassie has been badly guided all her life, and as she would not be ruled by the rudder, she must be ruled by the rocks."

"Think shame of yourself! forespeaking ill to a new-made bride! How would you like me to say such words to Christina?"

"Christina would never give occasion for them. She is as true as steel to her own lad."

"Maybe she has no temptation to be false. That makes a deal of differ. Anyway, Sophy is a woman now in the married state, and answerable to none but her husband. I hope Andrew is not fretting more than might be expected."

"Andrew! Andrew fretting! Not he! Not a minute! As soon as he knew she was a wife, he cast her out of his very thoughts. You don't catch Andrew Binnie putting a light-of-love lassie before a command of God."

"I won't hear you talk of my niece — of the mistress of Braelands — in that kind of a way,

Janet. She's our betters now, and we be to take notice of the fact."

"She'll have to learn and unlearn a good lot before she is to be spoke of as any one's 'betters.' I hope while she is seeing the world she will get her eyes opened to her own faults; they will give her plenty to think of."

"Keep me, woman! Such a way to go on about your own kin."

"She is no kin to the Binnies. I have cast her out of my reckoning."

"She is Christina's sixth cousin."

"She is nothing at all to us. I never did set any store by those Orkney folks — a bad lot! A very selfish, false, bad lot!"

"You are speaking of my people, Janet."

"I am quite aware of it, Griselda."

"Then keep your tongue in bounds."

"My tongue is my own."

"My house is my own. And if you can't be civil, I'll be necessitated to ask you to leave it."

"I'm going as soon as I have told you that you have the most gun-powdery temper I ever came across; forbye, you are fairly drunk with the conceit and vanity of Sophy's grand marriage. You are full as the Baltic with the pride of it, woman!"

"Temper! It is you, that are in a temper."

" That's neither here nor there. I have my reasons."

" Reasons, indeed! I'd like to see you reasonable for once."

" Yes, I have my reasons. How was my lad Andrew used by the both of you? And what do you think of his last meeting with that heartless limmer and her fine sweetheart? "

" Andrew should have kept himself out of their way. As soon as Braelands came round Sophy, Andrew got the very de'il in him. I was aye feared there would be murder laid to his name."

" You need n't have been feared for the like of that. Andrew Binnie has enough of the devil in him to keep the devil out of him. Do you think he would put blood on his soul for Sophy Traill? No, not for twenty lasses better than her! You need n't look at me as if your eyes were cocked pistols. I have heard all I wanted to hear, and said all I wanted to say, and now I'll be stepping homeward."

" I'll be obligated to you to go at once — the sooner the better."

" And I'll never speak to you again in this world, Griselda; nor in the next world either, unless you mend your manners. Mind that! "

" You are just full of envy, and all uncharitableness, and evil speaking, Janet Binnie. But

I trust I have more of the grace of God about me than to return your ill words. "

" That may be. It only shows folk that the grace of God will bide with an old woman that no one else can bide with."

" Old woman ! I am twenty years younger — "

But Janet had passed out of the room and clashed the shop door behind her with a pealing ring; so Griselda's little scream of indignation never reached her. It is likely, however, she anticipated the words that followed her, for she went down the street, folding her shawl over her ample chest, and smiling the smile of those who have thrown the last word of offence.

She did not reach home until quite dark, for she was stopped frequently by little groups of the wives and maids of Pittenduric, who wanted to hear the news about Sophy. It pleased Janet, for some reason, to magnify the girl's position and all the fine things it had brought her. Perhaps, because she felt dimly that it placed Andrew's defeat in a better light. No one could expect a mere fisherman to have any chance against a man able to shower silks and satins and gold and jewels upon his bride, and who could take her to France and Italy and Germany, not to speak of Asia and America.

But if this was her motive, it was a bit of
motherhood thrown away. Andrew had sources
of comfort and vindication which looked far
beyond all petty social opinion. He was on the
sea alone till nearly dark; then he came home,
with the old grave smile on his face, saying, as
he entered the house, " There will be a heavy
blow from the northeast to-night, Christina. I
see the boats are all at anchor, and no prospect
of a fishing."

" Ay, and I saw the birds, who know more
than we do, making for the rocks. I wish mother
would come," — and she opened the door and
looked out into the dark vacancy. " There is
a voice in the sea to-night, Andrew, and I don't
like the wail of it."

But Andrew had gone to his room, and so
she left the door open until Janet returned.
And the first question Janet asked was concerning Andrew. " Has he come home yet,
Christina? I'm feared for a boat on the sea
to-night."

" He is home, and I think he has fallen asleep.
He looked very tired."

" How is he taking his trouble ? "

" Like a man. Like himself. He has had
his wrestle out on the sea, and has come out
with a victory."

" The Lord be thanked ! Now, Christina,

I have heard everything about that wicked lassie. Let us have a cup of tea and a herring — for it is little good I had of Griselda's wishy-washy brew — and then I'll tell you the news of the wedding, the beginning and the end of it."

CHAPTER VI

WHERE IS MY MONEY?

IN the morning it was still more evident that Andrew had thrown himself on God, and — unperplext seeking, had found him. But Janet wondered a little that he did not more demonstratively seek the comfort of The Book. It was her way in sorrow to appeal immediately to its known passages of promise and comfort; and she laid it open in his way with the remark:

" There is the Bible, Andrew; it will have a word, no doubt, for you."

" And there is the something beyond the Bible. Mother, if you will be seeking it. When the Lord God speaks to a man, he has the perfection of counsel, and he will not be requiring the word of a prophet or an apostle. From the heart of The Unseen a voice calls to him, and gives him patience under suffering. I *know*, for I have heard and answered it." Then he walked to the door, and opening it, he stood there repeating to himself, as he looked over the waters which had been the field of his conflict and his victory: —

"But peace they have that none may gain that live;
And rest about them that no love can give:
And over them, while death and life shall be,
The light and sound and darkness of the Sea."

It was a verse that meant more to Andrew than he would have been able to explain. He only knew that it led him somehow through those dim, obscure pathways of spiritual life, on which the light of common day does not shine. And as he stood there, his mother and sister felt vaguely that they knew what "moral beauty" meant, and were the better for the knowledge.

He did not try to forget Sophy; he only placed her beyond his own horizon; and whereas he had once thought of her with personal hope and desire, he now remembered her only with a prayer for her happiness, or if by chance his tongue spoke her name, he added a blessing with it. Never did he make a complaint of her desertion, but he wept inwardly; and it was easy to see that he spent many of those hours that make the heart grey, though they leave the hair untouched. And it was at this time he contracted the habit of frequently looking up, finding in the very act that sense of strength and help and adoration which is inseparable to it. And thus, day by day, he overcame the aching sorrow of his heart, for no man is ever crushed from without; if he is abased to despair, his ruin has come from within.

About three weeks after Sophy's marriage, Christina was standing one evening at the gloaming, looking over the immense, cheerless waste of waters. Mists, vague and troublous as the background of dreams, were on the horizon; and there was a feeling of melancholy in the air. But she liked the damp, fresh wind, with its taste of brine, and she drew her plaid round her, and breathed it with a sense of enjoyment. Very soon Andrew came up the cliff; and he stood at her side, and they spoke of Jamie and wondered at his whereabouts, and after a little pause, Andrew added: —

"Christina, I got a very important letter to-day, and I am going to-morrow about the business I told you of. I want to start early in the morning, so put up what I need in my little bag. And I wish you to say nothing to mother until all things are settled."

"She will maybe ask me the question, Andrew."

"I told her I was going about a new boat, and she took me at my word without this or that to it. She is a blithe creature, one of the Lord's most contented bairns. I wish we were both more like her."

"I wish we were, Andrew. If we could just

do as mother does! for she leaves yesterday where it fell, and trusts to-morrow with God, and so catches every blink of happiness that passes by her."

" God forever bless her! There is no mother like the mother that bore us; we must aye remember that, Christina. But it is a dour, storm-like sky yon," he continued, pointing eastward. "We shall have a snoring breeze before midnight."

Then Christina thought of her lover again, and as they turned in to the fireside, she began to tell her brother her hopes and fears about Jamie, and to read him portions of a letter received that day from America. While Andrew's trouble had been fresh and heavy on him, Christina had refrained herself from all speech about her lover; she felt instinctively that it would not be welcome and perhaps hardly kind. But this night it fell out naturally, and Andrew listened kindly and made his sister very happy by his interest in all that related to Jamie's future. Then he ate some bread and cheese with the women, and after the exercise went to his room, for he had many things to prepare for his journey on the following day.

Janet continued the conversation. It related to her daughter's marriage and settlement in Glasgow, and of this subject she never wearied.

The storm Andrew had foreseen was by this time raging round the cottage, the blustering waves making strange noises on the sands and falling on the rocks with a keen, lashing sound. It affected them gradually; their hearts became troubled, and they spoke low and with sad inflections, for both were thinking of the sailor-men and fishermen peopling the lonely waters.

"I wouldn't put out to sea this night," said Janet. "No, not for a capful of sovereigns."

"Yet there will be plenty of boats, hammering through the big waves all night long, till the dawn shows in the east; and it is very like that Jamie is now on the Atlantic — a stormy place, God knows!"

"A good passage, if it so pleases God!" said Janet, lifting her eyes to heaven, and Christina looked kindly at her mother for the wish. But talking was fast becoming difficult, for the wind had suddenly veered more northerly, and, sleet-laden, it howled and shrieked down the wide chimney. In one of the pauses forced on them by this blatant intruder, they were startled by a human cry, loud and piercing, and quite distinct from the turbulent roar of winds and waves.

Both women were on their feet on the instant. Both had received the same swift, positive impression, that it came from Andrew's room, and they were at his door in a moment. It was locked. They called him, and he made no answer. Again and again, with ever increasing terror, they entreated him to open to them; for the door was solid and heavy, and the lock large and strong, and no power they possessed could avail to force an entrance. He heeded none of their passionate prayers until Janet began to cry bitterly. Then he turned the key and they entered.

Andrew looked at them with anger; his countenance was pale and distraught, and a quiet fury burned in his eyes. He could not speak, and the women regarded him with fear and wonder. Presently he managed to articulate with a thick difficulty: —

" My money! My money! It is all gone! "

" Gone! " shrieked Christina, " that is just impossible."

" It is all gone ! " Then he gripped her cruelly by the shoulder, and asked in a fierce whisper:

" What did you do with it ? "

" Me? Andrew ! "

" Ay, you ! You wicked lass, you ! "

" I never put finger on it."

" Christina ! Christina ! To think that I trusted you for this ! Go out of my sight, will you ! I 'm not able to bear the face of you ! "

" Andrew ! Andrew ! Surely, you are not calling me a ' thief ' ? "

" Who, then ? " he cried, with gathering rage, " unless it be Jamie Logan ? "

" Don't be so wicked as to wrong innocent folk such a way; Jamie never saw, never heard tell of your money. The unborn babe is not more guiltless than Jamie Logan."

" How do *you* know that? How do *I* know that? The very night I told you of the money — that very night I showed you where I kept it — that night Jamie ought to have been in the boats, and he was not in them. What do you make of that? "

" Nothing. He is as innocent as I am."

" And he was drinking with some strange man at the 'public.' What were they up to? Tell me that. And then he comes whistling up the road, and says he missed his boat. A made up story! and after it he goes off to America! Oh, woman! woman! If you can't put facts together, I can."

" Jamie never touched a bawbee of your money. I'll ware my life on that. For I never let on to any mortal creature that you had a penny of silent money. God Almighty knows I am speaking the truth."

" You won't dare to bring God Almighty's name into such a black business. Are you not feared to take it into your mouth? "

Then Janet laid her hand heavily on his

shoulder. He had sat down on his bed, and was leaning heavily against one of the posts, and the very fashion of his countenance was changed ; his hair stood upright, and he continually smote his large, nervous hands together.

"Andrew," said his mother, angrily, "you are just giving yourself up to Satan. Your passion is beyond seeing, or hearing tell of. And think shame of yourself for calling your sister a ' thief' and a 'liar' and what not. I wonder what 's come over you ! Step ben the house, and talk reasonable to us."

"Leave me to myself! Leave me to myself! I tell you both to go away. Will you go? both of you?"

"I 'm your mother, Andrew."

"Then for God's sake have pity on me, and leave me alone with my sorrow ! Go ! Go ! I 'm not a responsible creature just now —" and his passion was so stern and terrific that neither of them dared to face any increase of it.

So they left him alone and went back to the sputtering fireside — for the rain was now beating down the chimney — and in awe-struck whispers Christina told her mother of the money which Andrew had hoarded through long laborious years, and of the plans which the loss of it would break to pieces.

"There would be a thousand pounds, or near

by it, Mother, I'm thinking," said Christina.
" You know well how scrimping with himself
he has been. Good fishing or bad fishing, he
never had a shilling to spend on any one. He
bought nothing other boys bought; when he
was a laddie, and when he grew to the boats,
you may mind that he put all he made away
somewhere. And he made a deal more than
folks thought. He had a bit venture here, and
a bit there, and they must have prospered
finely."

" Not they ! " said Janet angrily. " What
good has come of them? What good *could*
come of money, hid away from everybody but
himself? Why did n't he tell his mother ? If
her thoughts had been round about his siller,
it would not have gone an ill road. A man who
hides away his money is just a miracle of stupid-
ity, for the devil knows where it is if no decent
human soul does."

It was a mighty sorrow to bear, even for the
two women, and Janet wept like a child over
the hopes blasted before she knew of them.
" He should have told us both long since," she
sobbed. " I would have been praying for the
bonnie ship building for him, every plank would
have been laid with a blessing. And as I sat quiet
in my house, I would have been thinking of my
son Captain Binnie, and many a day would have

been a bright day, that has been but a middling one. So selfish as the lad has been!"

"Maybe it wasn't pure selfishness, Mother. He was saving for a good end."

"It was pure selfishness! He was that way even about Sophy. Nobody but himself must have word or look from her, and the lassie just wearied of him. Why wouldn't she? He put himself and her in a circle, and then made a wilderness all round about it. And Sophy wanted company, for when a girl says 'a man is all the world to her,' she doesn't mean that nobody else is to come into her world. She would be a wicked lass if she did."

"Well, Mother, he lost her, and he bore his loss like a man."

"Ay, men often bear the loss of love easier than the loss of money. I've seen far more fuss made over the loss of a set of fishing-nets, than over the brave fellows that handled them. And to think of our Andrew hiding away his gold all these years for his own hoping and pleasuring! A perfectly selfish pleasuring! The gold might well take wings to itself and fly away. He should have clipped the wings of it with giving a piece to the kirk now and then, and a piece to his mother and sister at odd times, and the flying wouldn't have been so easy. Now he has lost the whole, and he well deserves it. I'm thinking his Maker is dourly angry with him for such ways, and I am angry myself."

"Ah well, Mother, there is no use in our anger; the lad is suffering enough, and for the rest we must just leave him to the general mercy of God."

"'General mercy of God.' Don't let me hear you use the like of such words, Christina. The minister would tell you it is a very loose expression and a very dangerous doctrine. He was reproving Elder McInnes for them very words, and any good minister will be keeping his thumb on such a wide outgate. Andrew knows well that he has to have the particular and elected grace of God to keep him where he ought to be. This hid-away money has given him a sore tumble, and I will tell him so very plainly."

"Don't trouble him, Mother. He will not bear words on it, even from you."

"He will have to bear them. I am not feared for Andrew Binnie, and he shall not be left in ignorance of his sin. Whether he knows it or not, he has done a deed that would make a very poor kind of a Christian ashamed to look the devil in the face; and I be to let him know it."

But in the morning Andrew looked so utterly wretched, that Janet could only pity him. "I'll not be the one to break the bruised reed," she

said to Christina, for the miserable man sat silent
with dropped eyes the whole day long, eating
nothing, seeing nothing, and apparently lost to
all interests outside his own bewildering, utterly
hopeless speculations. It was not until another
letter came about the ship he was to command,
that he roused himself sufficiently to write and
cancel the whole transaction. He could not
keep his promises financially, and though he
was urged to make some other offer, he would
have nothing from The Fleet on any humbler
basis than his first proposition. With a foolish
pride, born of his great disappointment and
anger, he turned his back on his broken hopes,
and went sullen and sorrowful back to his fishing-boat.

He had never been even in his family a very
social man. Jokes and songs and daffing of all
kinds were alien to his nature. Yet his grave
and pleasant smile had been a familiar thing,
and gentle words had always hitherto come
readily to his lips. But after his ruinous loss,
he seldom spoke unless it was to his mother.
Christina he noticed not, either by word or
look, and the poor girl was broken-hearted
under this silent accusation. For she felt that
Andrew doubted both her and Jamie, and
though she was indignant at the suspicion, it eat
its way into her heart and tortured her.

For put the thought away as she would, the fact of Jamie's dereliction that unfortunate night would return and return, and always with a more suspicious aspect. Who was the man he was drinking with? Nobody in the village, but Jamie, knew him. He had come and gone in a night. It was possible that, having missed the boat, Jamie had brought his friend up the cliff to call on her; that, seeing the light in Andrew's room, they had looked in at the window, and so might have seen Andrew and herself standing over the money, and then watched until it was returned to its hiding-place. Jamie *had* come whistling in a very pronounced manner up to the house — that might have been because he had been drinking, and then again, it might not — and then there was his quarrel with Andrew! Was that a planned affair, in order to give the other man time to carry off the box? She could not remember whether the curtain had been drawn across the window or not; and when she dared to name this doubt to Andrew, he only answered : —

"What for are you asking after spilled milk?"

The whole circumstance was so mysterious that it stupified her. And yet she felt that it contained all the elements of sorrow and separation between Jamie and herself. However, she kept assuring her heart that Jamie would be in

Glasgow the following week; and she wrote a letter to meet him, expressing a strong desire that he would " be sure to come to Pittendurie, as there was most important business." But she did not like to tell him what the business was, and Jamie did not answer the request. In fact, the lad could not, without resigning his position entirely. The ship had been delayed thirty hours by storms, and there was nearly double tides of work for every man on her in order that she might be able to keep her next sailing day. Jamie was therefore so certain that a request to go on shore about his own concerns would be denied, that he did not even ask the favour.

But he wrote to Christina, and explained to her in the most loving manner the impossibility of his leaving his duties. He said " that for her sake, as well as his own, he was obligated to remain at his post," and he assured her that this obligation was " a reasonable one." Christina believed him fully, and was satisfied; her mother only smiled with shut lips and remained silent; but Andrew spoke with a bitterness it was hard to forgive; still harder was it to escape from the wretched inferences his words implied.

"No wonder he keeps away from Pittendurie!" he said with a scornful laugh. "He'll come here no more — unless he is made to come; and if it was not for mother's sake, and for your

good name, Christina, I would send the con-
stables to the ship to bring him here this very
day."

And Christina could make no answer, save
that of passionate weeping. For it shocked her
to see, that her mother did not stand up for
Jamie, but went silently about her house duties,
with a face as inscrutable as the figure-head of
Andrew's boat.

Thus backward, every way, flew the wheels of
life in the Binnie cottage. Andrew took a grim
pleasure in accepting his poverty before his
mother and sister. In the home he made them
feel that everything but the barest necessities
were impossible wants. His newspaper was
resigned; his pipe also, after a little struggle.
He took his tea without sugar; he put the butter
and marmalade aside, as if they were sinful
luxuries; and in fact reduced his life to the
most essential and primitive conditions it was
possible to live it on. And as Janet and Christina were not the bread winners, and did not
know the exact state of the Binnie finances, they
felt obliged to follow Andrew's example. Of
course, all Christina's little extravagances of
wedding preparations were peremptorily stopped.
There would be no silk wedding-gown now. It
began to look, as if there would be no wedding
at all.

For Andrew's continual suspicions, spoken and unspoken, insensibly affected her ; and that in spite of her angry denials of them. She fought against their influence, but often in vain ; for Jamie did not come to Pittendurie either after the second or the third voyage. He was not to blame ; it was the winter season, and delays were constant, and there were other circumstances — with which he had nothing whatever to do — that still put him in such a position that to ask for leave of absence meant asking for his dismissal. And then there would be no prospect at all of his marriage with Christina.

But the fisher folk, who had their time very much at their own command, and who were nursed in a sense of every individual's independence, did not realise Jamie's dilemma. It could not be made intelligent to them, and they began to wonder, and to ask embarrassing questions. Very soon there was a shake of the head and a sigh of pity whenever " poor Christina Binnie " was mentioned.

So four wretched months went by, and then one moonlight night in February, Christina heard the quick footstep and the joyous whistle she knew so well. She stood up trembling with pleasure ; and as Jamie flung wide the door, she flew to his arms with an irrepressible cry. For some minutes he saw nothing and

135

cared for nothing but the girl clasped to his breast; but as she began to sob, he looked at Janet — who had purposely gone to the china rack that she might have her back to him — and then at Andrew who stood white and stern, with both hands in his pockets, regarding him.

The young man was confounded by this reception; he released himself from Chistina's embrace, and stepping forward, asked anxiously: "What ever is the matter with you, Andrew? You aren't like yourself at all. Why, you are ill, man! Oh, but I'm vexed to see you so changed."

"Where is my money, James Logan? Where is the gold and the bank-notes you took from me? — the savings of all my lifetime."

"Your money, Andrew? Your gold and bank-notes? *Me* take your money! Why, man, you are either mad or joking — and I'm not liking such jokes either." Then he turned to Christina and asked, "What does he mean, my dearie?"

"I mean this," cried Andrew with gathering passion, "I mean that I had nearly a thousand pounds taken out of my room yon night that you should have gone to the boats — and that you did *not* go."

"Do you intend to say that I took your thousand pounds? Mind your words, Andrew

Binnie!" and as he spoke, he put Christina behind him and stood squarely before Andrew. And his face was a flame of passion.

"I am most sure you took it. Prove to me that you did not."

Before the words were finished, they were answered with a blow; the blow was promptly returned; and then the two men closed in a deadly struggle. Christina was white and sick with terror, but withal glad that Andrew had found himself so promptly answered. Janet turned sharply at the first blow, and threw herself between the men. All the old prowess of the fish-wife was roused in her.

"How dare you?" she cried in a temper quite equal to their own. "I'll have no cursing and fighting in my house;" and with a twist of her hand in her son's collar, she threw him back in his chair. Then she turned to Jamie and cried angrily: —

"Jamie Logan, my bonnie lad, if you have got nothing to say for yourself, you'll do well to take your way down the cliff."

"I have been called a 'thief' in this house," he answered; and wounded feeling and a bitter sense of wrong made his voice tremble. "I came here to kiss my bride; and I know nothing at all of what Andrew means. I will swear it. Give me the Bible."

"Let my Bible alone," shouted Andrew. "I'll have no man swear to a lie on my Bible. Get out of my house, James Logan; and be thankful that I don't call the officers to take care of you."

"There is a mad man inside of you, Andrew Binnie, or a devil of some kind, and you are not fit to be in the same house with good women. Come with me, Christina. I'll marry you to-night at the Largo minister's house. Come, my dear lassie. Never mind aught you have, but your plaidie."

Christina rose and put out her hand. Andrew leaped to his feet and strode between them.

"I will strike you to the ground, if you dare to touch my sister again," he shouted, and if Janet had not taken both his hands in her own strong grip, Andrew would have kept his threat. Then Janet's anger turned most unreasonably upon Christina —

"Go ben the house," she screamed. "Go ben the house, you worrying, whimpering lassie. You will be having the whole village fighting about you the next thing."

"I am going with Jamie, Mother."

"I will take very good care, you do *not* go with Jamie. There is not a soul, but Jamie Logan, will leave this house to-night. I would just like to see any other man or woman try it," and she looked defiantly both at Andrew and Christina.

"I ran the risk of losing my berth to come here," said Jamie. "More fool, I. I have been called 'thief' and 'loon' for doing it. I came for your sake, Christina, and now you must go with me for my sake. Come away, my dearie, and there is none that shall part us more."

Again Christina rose, and again her mother interfered. "You will go out of this house alone, Jamie Logan. I don't know whether you are right or wrong. I know nothing about that weary siller. But I do know there has been nothing but trouble to my boy since he saved you from the sea. I am not saying it is your fault; but the sea has been against him ever since, and now you will go away, and you will stay away."

"Christina, am I to go?"

"Go, Jamie, but I will come to you, and there is none that shall keep me from you."

Then Jamie went, and far down on the sands Christina heard him call, "Good-bye, Christina! Good-bye!" And she would have answered him, but Janet had locked the door, and the key was in her pocket. Then for hours the domestic storm raged, Andrew growing more and more positive and passionate, until even Janet was alarmed, and with tears and coaxing persuaded him to go to bed. Still in this hurly-burly of temper, Christina kept her purpose intact. She was determined to go to Glasgow as soon as she could get outside. If she was in time for a marriage with Jamie, she would be his wife at once. If Jamie had gone, then she would hire herself out until the return of his ship.

This was the purpose she intended to carry out in the morning; but before the dawn her mother awakened her out of a deep sleep. She was in a sweat of terror.

"Run up the cliff for Thomas Roy," she cried, "and then send Sandy for the doctor."

"What is the matter, Mother."

"Your brother Andrew is raving, and clean beyond himself; and I'm feared for him, and for us all. Quick Christina! There is not a moment to lose!"

CHAPTER VII

THE BEGINNING OF THE END

ON this same night the Mistress of Braelands sat musing by the glowing bit of fire in her bedroom, while her maid, Allister, was folding away her silk dinner-gown, and making the preparations for the night's toilet. She was a stately, stern-looking woman, with that air of authority which comes from long and recognised position. Her dressing-gown of pale blue flannel fell amply around her tall form; her white hair was still coiled and puffed in an elaborate fashion, and there was at the wrist-bands of her sleeves a fall of lace which half covered her long, shapely white hands. She was pinching its plaits mechanically, and watching the effect as she idly turned them in the firelight to catch the gleam of opal and amethyst rings. But this accompaniment to her thoughts was hardly a conscious one; she had admired her hands for so many years that she was very apt to give to their beauty this homage of involuntary observation, even when her thoughts were fixed on subjects far-off and alien to them.

141

" Allister," she said, suddenly, " I wonder where Mr. Archibald will be this night."

" The Lord knows, Madame, and it is well he does; for it is little we know of ourselves and the ways we walk in."

" The Lord looks after his own, Allister, and Mr. Archibald was given to him by kirk and parents before he was a month old. But if a man marries such a woman as you know nothing about, and then goes her ways, what will you say then? "

" It is not as bad as that, Madame. Mrs. Archibald is of well-known people, though poor."

" Though low-born, Allister. Poverty can be tholed, and even respected; but for low birth there is no remedy but being born over again."

" Well, Madame, she is Braelands now, and that is a cloak to cover all defects; and if I was you I would just see that it did so."

" She is my son's wife, and must be held as such, both by gentle and simple."

" And there is few ills that have not a good side to them, Madame. If Mr. Archibald had married Miss Roberta Elgin, as you once feared he would do, there would have been a flitting for you and for me, Madame. Miss Roberta would have had the whole of Braelands House to herself, and the twenty-two rooms of it would n't have been enough for her. And she would have taken the Braelands's honour and glory on her own shoulders. It would have been 'Mrs. Archibald Braelands' here and there and everywhere, and you would have been pushed out of sight and hearing, and passed by altogether, like as not; for if youth and beauty and wealth and good blood set themselves to have things their own way, which way at all will age that is not rich keep for itself? Sure as death, Madame, you would have had to go to the Dower House, which is but a mean little place, though big enough, no doubt, for all the friends and acquaintances that would have troubled themselves to know you there."

"You are not complimentary, Allister. I think I have few friends who would *not* have followed me to the Dower House."

"Surely, Madame, you may as well think so. But carriages aye stop at big houses; indeed, the very coachmen and footmen and horses are dead set against calling at cottages. There is many a lady who would be feared to ask her coachman to call at the Dower House. But what for am I talking? There is no occasion to think that Mrs. Archibald will ever dream of sending you out of this house."

"I came here a bride, nearly forty years ago, Allister," she said, with a touch of sentimental pity for herself in the remembrance.

" So you have had a long lease, Madame, and one like to be longer; for never a better son than your son; and I do think for sure that the lady he has married will be as biddable as a very child with you."

" I hope so. For she will have everything to learn about society, and who can teach her better than I can, Allister? "

" No one, Madame; and Mrs. Archibald was ever good at the uptake. I am very sure if you will show her this and that, and give her the word here and there yourself, Madame, there will be no finer lady in Fife before the year has come and gone. And she cannot be travelling with Mr. Archibald without learning many a thing all the winter long."

" Yes, they will not be home before the spring, I hear."

" And oh, Madame, by that date you will have forgot that all was not as you wanted it! And no doubt you will give the young things the loving welcome they are certain to be longing for."

" I do not know, Allister. The marriage was a great sorrow, and shame, and disappointment to me. I am not sure that I have forgiven it."

" Lady Beith was saying you never would forgive it. She was saying that you could never forgive any one's faults but your own."

" Lady Beith is very impertinent. And pray what faults has Lady Beith ever seen in me?"

" It was her general way of speaking, Madame. She has that way."

" Then you might tell Lady Beith's woman, that such general ways of speaking are ex-- tremely vulgar. When her ladyship speaks of the Mistress of Braelands again, I will ask her to refer to me, particularly. I have my own virtues as well as my own faults, and my own position, and my own influence, and I do not go into the generalities of life. I am the Mistress of Braelands yet, I hope."

" I hope so, Madame. As I was saying, Mrs. Archibald is biddable as a child; but then again, she is quite capable of taking the rudder into her own hands, and driving in the teeth of the wind. You can't ever be sure of fisher blood. It is like the ocean, whiles calm as a sleeping baby, whiles lashing itself into a very fury. There is both this and that in the Traills, and Mrs. Archibald is one of them."

" Any way and every way, this marriage is a great sorrow to me."

" I am not disputing that, Madame; but I am sure you remember what the minister was saying to you at his last visitation — that every sorrow you got the mastery over was a benefactor."

"The minister is not always orthodox, Allister."

"He is a very good man; every one is saying that."

"No doubt, no doubt, but he deviates."

"Well then, Madame, even if the marriage be as bad as you fancy it, bad things as well as good ones come to an end, and life, after all, is like a bit of poetry I picked up somewhere, which says:

> 'There's nane exempt frae worldly cares;
> And few frae some domestic jars;
> Whyles *all* are in, whyles *all* are out,
> And grief and joy come turn about.'

And it's the turn now for the young people to be happy. Cold and bleak it is here on the Fife coast, but they are among roses and sunshine; and so God bless them, I say, and keep us and every one from cutting short their 'turn' of happiness. You had your bride-time, Madame, and when Angus McAllister first took me to his cottage in Strathmoyer, I thought I was on a visit to Paradise."

"Give me my glass of negus, and then I will go to bed. Everybody has taken to preaching and advising lately, and that is not the kind of fore-talk that spares after-talk — not it, Allister."

She sunk then into unapproachable silence,

and Allister knew that she needed not try to move her further that night in any direction. Her eyes were fixed upon the red coals, but she was really thinking of the roses and sunshine of the South, and picturing to herself her son and his bride, wandering happily amid the warmth and beauty.

In reality, they were crossing the Braelands's moor at that very moment. The rain was beating against the closed windows of their coach, and the horses floundering heavily along the boggy road. Sophy's head rested on her husband's shoulder, but they were not talking, nor had they spoken for some time. Both indeed were tired and depressed, and Archie at least was unpleasantly conscious of the wonderment their unexpected return would cause.

The end of April or the beginning of May had been the time appointed, and yet here they were, at the threshold of their home, in the middle of the winter. Sophy's frail health had been Archie's excuse for a season in the South with her; and she was coming back to Scotland when the weather was at its very bleakest and coldest. One excuse after another formed itself in Archie's mind, only to be peremptorily dismissed. " It is no one's business but our own," he kept assuring himself, "and I will give neither reason nor apology but my wife's desire ; " and yet he knew that reasons and apologies would be asked, and he was fretting inwardly at their necessity, and wondering vaguely if women ever did know what they really wanted.

For to go to France and Germany and Italy, had seemed to Sophy the very essence of every joy in life. Before her marriage, she had sat by Archie's side hour after hour, listening to his descriptions of foreign lands, and dreaming of all the delights that were to meet her in them. She had started on this bridal trip with all her senses set to an unnatural key of expectation, and she had, of course, suffered continual disappointments and disillusions. The small frets and sicknesses of travel; the loneliness of being in places where she could not speak even to her servants, or go shopping without an attendant; the continual presence of what was strange — of what wounded her prejudices and very often her conscience ; — and the constant absence of all that was familiar and approved, were in themselves no slight cause of unhappiness.

Yet it had been a very gradual disillusion, and one mitigated by many experiences that had fully justified even Sophy's extravagant anticipations. The trouble, in the main, was one common to a great majority of travellers for pleasure — a mind totally unprepared for the experience.

She grew weary of great cities which had no individual character or history in her mind; weary of fine hotels in which she was of no special importance; weary of art which had no meaning for her. Her child-like enthusiasms, which at first both delighted and embarrassed her husband, faded gradually away; the present not only lost its charm, but she began to look backward to the homely airs and scenes of Fife, and to suffer from a nostalgia that grew worse continually.

However, Archie bore her unreasonable depression with great consideration. She was but a frail child after all, and she was in a condition of health demanding the most affectionate patience and tenderness he could give her. Besides, it was no great sin in his eyes to be sick with longing for dear old Scotland. He loved his native land; and his little mountain blue-bell, trembling in every breeze, and drooping in every hour of heat and sunshine, appealed to the very best instincts of his nature. And when Sophy began to voice her longing, to cry a little in his arms, and to say she was wearying for a sight of the great grey sea round her Fife home, Archie vowed he was homesick as a man could be, and asked, " why they should stop away from their own dear land any longer?"

" People will wonder and talk so, Archie
They will say unkind things — they will maybe
say we are not happy together."

" Let them talk. What care we? And we
are happy together. Do you want to go back
to Scotland to-morrow? to-day — this very
hour?"

" Aye, I do, Archie. And I am that weak
and poorly, if I don't go soon, maybe I will
have to wait a long time, and then you know—"

" Yes, I know. And that would never, never
do. Braelands of Fife cannot run the risk of
having his heir born in a foreign country. Why,
it would be thrown up to the child, lad and
man, as long as he lived! So call your maid,
my bonnie Sophy, and set her to packing all
your braws and pretty things, and we will turn
our faces to Scotland's hills and braes to-morrow
morning."

Thus it happened that on that bleak night in
February, Archie Braelands and his wife came
suddenly to their home, amid the stormy winds
and rains of a stormy night. Madame heard
the wheels of their carriage as she sat sipping
her negus, and thinking over her conversation
with Allister; and her alert soul instantly divined
who the late comers were.

" Give me my silk morning gown and my
brocade petticoat, Allister," she cried, as she

rose up hastily and set down her glass. "Mr. Archibald has come home; his carriage is at the door — haste ye, woman!"

"Will you be heeding your silks to-night, Madame?"

"Get them at once. Quick! Do you think I will meet the bride in a flannel dressing-gown? No, no! I am not going to lose ground the first hour."

With nervous haste the richer garments were donned, and just as the final gold brooch was clasped, Archie knocked at his mother's door. She opened to him with her own hands, and took him to her heart with an effusive affection she rarely permitted herself to exhibit.

"I am so glad that you are dressed, Mother," he said. "Sophy must not miss your welcome, and the poor little woman is just weary to death." Then he whispered some words to her, which brought a flush of pride and joy to his own face, but no such answering response to Madame's.

"Indeed," she replied, "I am sorry she is so tired. It seems to me, that the women of this generation are but weak creatures."

Then she took her son's arm, and went down to the parlour, where servants were re-kindling the fire, and setting a table with refreshments for the unexpected guests. Sophy was resting on a sofa drawn towards the hearth. Archie had thrown his travelling-cloak of black fox over her, and her white, flower-like face, surrounded by the black fur, had a singularly pathetic beauty. She opened her large blue eyes as Madame approached, and looked at her with wistful entreaty; and Madame, in spite of all her pre-arrangements of conduct, was unable at that hour not to answer the appeal for affection she saw in them. She stooped and kissed the child-like little woman, and Archie watched this token of reconciliation and promise with eyes wet with happiness.

When supper was served, Madame took her usual place at the head of the table, and Archie noticed the circumstance, though it did not seem a proper time to make any remark about it. For Sophy was not able to eat, and did not rise from her couch; and Madame seemed to fall so properly into her character of hostess, that it would have been churlish to have made the slightest dissent. Yet it was a false kindness to both; for in the morning Madame took the same position, and Archie felt less able than on the previous night to make any opposition, though he had told himself continually on his homeward journey that he would not suffer Sophy to be imposed upon, and would demand for her the utmost title of her rights as his wife.

In this resolve, however, he had forgot to take into account his mother's long and absolute influence over him. When she was absent, it was comparatively easy to relegate her to the position she ought to occupy; when she was present, he found it impossible to say or do anything which made her less than Mistress of Braelands. And during the first few weeks after her return, Sophy helped her mother-in-law considerably against herself. She was so anxious to please, so anxious to be loved, so afraid of making trouble for Archie, that she submitted without protest to one infringement after another on her rights as the wife of the Master of Braelands. All the same she was dumbly conscious of the wrong being done to her; and like a child, she nursed her sense of the injustice until it showed itself in a continual mood of sullen, silent protest.

After the lapse of a month or more, she became aware that even her ill health was used as a weapon against her, and she suddenly resolved to throw off her lassitude, and assert her right to go out and call upon her friends. But she was petulant and foolish in the carrying out of the measure. She had made up her mind to visit her aunt on the following day, and though the weather was bitterly cold and damp, she adhered to her resolution. Madame, at first politely, finally with provoking positiveness, told her " she would not permit her to risk her life, and a life still more precious, for any such folly."

Then Sophy rose, with a sudden excitement of manner, and rang the bell. When the servant appeared, she ordered the carriage to be ready for her in half an hour. Madame waited until they were alone, and then said : —

"Sophy, go to your room and lie down. You are not fit to go out. I shall counter-order the carriage in your name."

" You will not," cried the trembling, passionate girl. " You have ordered and counter-ordered in my name too much. You will, in the future, mind your own affairs, and leave me to attend to mine."

" When Archie comes back — "

" You will tell him all kinds of lies. I know that."

" I do not lie."

" Perhaps not; but you misrepresent things so, that you make it impossible for Archie to get at the truth. I want to see my aunt. You have kept me from her, and kept her from me, until I am sick for a sight of those who really love me. I am going to Aunt Kilgour's this very morning, whether you like it or not."

" You shall not leave this house until Archie

comes back from Largo. I will not take the responsibility."

"We shall see. *I* will take the responsibility myself. *I* am mistress of Braelands. You will please remember that fact. And I know my rights, though I have allowed you to take them from me."

"Sophy, listen to me."

"I am going to Aunt Kilgour's."

"Archie will be very angry."

"Not if you will let him judge for himself. Anyway, I don't care. I am going to see my aunt! You expect Archie to be always thinking of feelings, and your likes and dislikes. I have just as good a right to care about my aunt's feelings. She was all the same as mother to me. I have been a wicked lassie not to have gone to her lang syne."

"Wicked lassie! Lang syne! I wish you would at least try to speak like a lady."

"I am not a lady. I am just one of God's fisher folk. I want to see my own kith and kin. I am going to do so."

"You are not — until your husband gives you permission."

"Permission! do you say? I will go on my own permission, Sophy Braelands's permission."

"It is a shame to take the horses out in such weather — and poor old Thomas."

" Shame or not, I shall take them out."

" Indeed, no ! I cannot permit you to make a fool and a laughing-stock of yourself." She rang the bell sharply and sent for the coachman. When he appeared, she said : —

" Thomas, I think the horses had better not go out this morning. It is bitterly cold, and there is a storm coming from the northeast. Do you not think so ? "

" It is a bad day, Madame, and like to be worse."

" Then we will not go out."

As Madame uttered the words, Sophy walked rapidly forward. All the passion of her Viking ancestors was in her face, which had undergone a sort of transfiguration. Her eyes flashed, her soft curly yellow hair seemed instinct with a strange life and brilliancy, and she said with an authority that struck Madame with amazement and fear : —

" Thomas, you will have the carriage at the door in fifteen minutes, exactly," and she drew out her little jewelled watch, and gave him the time with a smiling, invincible calmness.

Thomas looked from one woman to the other, and said, fretfully, " A man canna tak' twa contrary orders at the same minute o' time. What will I do in the case ? "

" You will do as I tell you, Thomas," said

Madame. " You have done so for twenty years. Have you come to any scath or wrong by it? "

" If the carriage is not at the door in fifteen minutes, you will leave Braelands this night, Thomas," said Sophy. " Listen! I give you fifteen minutes; after that I shall walk into Largo, and you can answer to your master for it. I am Mistress of Braelands. Don't forget that fact if you want to keep your place, Thomas."

She turned passionately away with the words, and left the room. In fifteen minutes she went to the front door in her cloak and hood, and the carriage was waiting there. " You will drive me to my aunt Kilgour's shop," she said with an air of reckless pride and defiance. It pleased her at that hour to humble herself to her low estate. And it pleased Thomas also that she had done so. His sympathy was with the fisher girl. He was delighted that she had at last found courage to assert herself, for Sophy's wrongs had been the staple talk of the kitchen-table and fireside.

" No born lady I ever saw," he said afterwards to the cook, " could have held her own better. It will be an even fight between them two now, and I will bet my shilling on fisherman Traill's girl."

" Madame has more wit, and more *hold-out*," answered the cook. " Mrs. Archibald is good for a spurt, but I 'll be bound she cried her eyes red at Griselda Kilgour's, and was as weak as a baby."

This opinion was a perfectly correct one. Once in her aunt's little back parlour, Sophy gave full sway to her childlike temper. She told all her wrongs, and was comforted by her kinswoman's interest and pity, and strengthened in her resolution to resist Madame's interference with her life. And then the small black teapot was warmed and filled, and Sophy begged for a herring and a bit of oatcake; and the two women sat close to one another, and Miss Kilgour told Sophy all the gossip and clash of gossip there had been about Christina Binnie and her lover, and how the marriage had been broken off, no one knowing just why, but many thinking that since Jamie Logan had got a place on " The Line," he was set on bettering himself with a girl something above the like of Christina Binnie.

And as they talked Helen Marr came into the shop for a yard of ribbon, and said it was the rumour all through Pittendurie, that Andrew Binnie was all but dead, and folks were laying all the blame upon the Mistress of Braelands, for that every one knew that Andrew had never held up his head an hour since her marriage. And though Miss Kilgour did not encourage this phase of gossip, yet the woman would persist in describing his sufferings, and the poverty

that had come to the Binnies with the loss of
their only bread-winner, and the doctors to pay,
and the medicine folks said they had not the
money to buy, and much more of the same sort,
which Sophy heard every word of, knowing also
that Helen Marr must have seen her carriage at
the door, and so, knowing of her presence, had
determined that she should hear it.

Certainly if Helen had wished to wound her
to the very heart, she succeeded. When Miss
Kilgour got rid of her customer, and came back
to Sophy, she found her with her face in the
pillow, sobbing passionately about the trouble
of her old friends. She did not name Andrew,
but the thought of his love and suffering hurt
her sorely, and she could not endure to think of
Janet's and Christina's long hardships and sorrow. For she knew well how much they would
blame her, and the thought of their anger, and
of her own apparent ingratitude, made her sick
with shame and grief. And as they talked of
this new trouble, and Sophy sent messages of
love and pity to Janet and Christina, the shop-
bell rung violently, and Sophy heard her husband's step, and in another moment he was at
her side, and quite inclined to be very angry
with her for venturing out in such miserable
weather.

Then Sophy seized her opportunity, and Miss

Kilgour left them alone for the explanation that was better to be made there than at Braelands. And for once Archie took his wife's part without reservation. He was not indeed ill-pleased that she had assumed her proper position, and when he slipped a crown into Thomas's hand, the man also knew that he had done wisely. Indeed there was something in the coachman's face and air which affected Madame unpleasantly, before she noticed that Sophy had returned in her husband's company, and that they were evidently on the most affectionate terms.

"I have lost this battle," she said to herself, and she wisely retreated to her own room, and had a nominal headache, and a very genuine heartache about the loss.

All day long Sophy was at an unnatural pitch, all day long she exerted herself, as she had not done for weeks and months, to entertain and keep her husband at her side, and all day long her pretty wifely triumph was bright and unbroken. The very servants took a delight in ministering to it, and Madame was not missed in a single item of the household routine. But about midnight there was a great and sudden change. Bells were frantically rung, lights flew about the house, and there was saddling of horses and riding in hot haste into Largo for any or all the doctors that could be found.

Then Madame came quietly from her seclusion, and resumed her place as head of the household, for the little mistress of one day lay in her chamber quite unconscious of her lost authority. Some twelve hours later, the hoped-for heir of Braelands was born, and died, and Sophy, on the very outermost shoal of life, felt the wash and murmur of that dark river which flows to the Eternal Sea.

It was no time to reproach the poor little wife, and yet Madame did not scruple to do so. " She had warned Sophy, — she had begged her not to go out — she had been insulted for endeavouring to prevent what had come to pass just as she had predicted." And in spite of Archie's love and pity, her continual regrets did finally influence him. He began to think he had been badly used, and to agree with Madame in her assertions that Sophy must be put under some restrictions, and subjected to some social instruction.

" The idea of the Braelands's carriage standing two hours at Griselda Kilgour's shop door ! All the town talking about it ! Every one wondering what had happened at Braelands, to drive your wife out of doors in such weather. All sorts of rumours about you and Sophy, and Griselda shaking her head and sighing and looking unspeakable things, just to keep the curiosity alive ;

and the crowds of gossiping women coming
and going to her shop. Many a cap and bonnet
has been sold to your name, Archie, no doubt;
and I can tell you my own cheeks are kept
burning with the shame of the whole affair!
And then this morning, the first thing she said
to me was, that she wanted to see her cousins
Isobel and Christina."

"She asked me also about them, Mother, and
really, I think she had better be humoured in this
matter. Our friends are not her friends."

"They ought to be."

"Let us be just. When has she had any
opportunity to make them so? She has seen
no one yet, — her health has been so bad — and
it did often look, Mother, as if you encouraged
her *not* to see callers."

"Perhaps I did, Archie. You cannot blame
me. Her manners are so crude, so exigent, so
effusive. She is so much pleased, or so indifferent about people; so glad to see them, or else
so careless as to how she treats them. You
have no idea what I suffered when Lady Blair
called, and insisted on meeting your wife. Of
course she pretended to fall in love with her, and
kissed, and petted, and flattered Sophy, until
the girl hardly knew what she was doing or saying. And as for 'saying,' she fell into broad
Scotch, as she always does when she is pleased

or excited, and Lady Blair professed herself charmed, and talked broad Scotch back to her. And I? I sat tingling with shame and annoyance, for I knew right well what mockeries and laughter Sophy was supplying Annette Blair with for her future visitors."

"I think you are wrong. Lady Blair is not at all ill-natured. She was herself a poor minister's daughter, and accustomed to go in and out of the fishers' cottages. I can imagine that she would really be charmed with Sophy."

"You can 'imagine' what you like; that will not alter the real state of the case; and if Sophy is ever to take her position as your wife, she must be prepared for it. Besides which, it will be a good thing to give her some new interests in life, for she must drop the old ones. About that there cannot be two opinions."

"What then do you propose, Mother?"

"I should get proper teachers for her. Her English education has been frightfully neglected; and she ought to learn music and French."

"She speaks French pretty well. I never saw any one pick up a language as cleverly as she did the few weeks we were in Paris."

"O, she is clever enough if she wants to be! There is a French woman teaching at Miss Linley's Seminary. She will perfect her. And I have heard she also plays well. It would be a good thing to engage her for Sophy, two or three hours a day. A teacher for grammar, history, writing, etc., is easily found. I myself will give her lessons in social etiquette, and in all things pertaining to the dignity and decorum which your wife ought to exhibit. Depend upon it, Archie, this routine is absolutely necessary. It will interest and occupy her idle hours, of which she has far too many; and it will wean her better than any other thing from her low, uncultivated relations."

"The poor little woman says she wants to be loved; that she is lonely when I am away; that no one but the servants care for her; that therefore she wants to see her cousins and kinsfolk."

"She does me a great injustice. I would love her if she would be reasonable — if she would only trust me. But idle hearts are lonely hearts, Archie. Tell her you wish her to study, and fit herself for the position you have raised her to. Surely the desire to please you ought to be enough. Do you know *who* this Christina Binnie is that she talks so continually about?"

"Her fourth or fifth cousin, I believe."

"She is the sister of the man you won Sophy from — the man whom you struck across the cheek with your whip. Now do you wish her to see Christina Binnie!"

"Yes, I do! Do you think I am jealous or

fearful of my wife? No, by Heaven! No! Sophy may be unlearned and unfashionable, but she is loyal and true; and if she wants to see her old lover and his sister, she has my full permission. As for the fisherman, he behaved very nobly. And I did not intend to strike him. It was an accident, and I shall apologise for it the first opportunity I have to do so."

" You are a fool, Archie Braelands."

" I am a husband, who knows his wife's heart and who trusts in it. And though I think you are quite right in your ideas about Sophy's education, I do not think you are right in objecting to her seeing her old friends. Every one in this bound of Fife knows that I married a fisher-girl. I never intend to be ashamed of the fact. If our social world will accept her as the representative of my honour and my family, I shall be obliged to the world. If it will not, I can live without its approval — having Sophy to love me and live with me. I counted all this cost before I married; you may be sure of that, Mother."

" You forgot, however, to take my honour and feelings into your consideration."

" I knew, Mother, that you were well able to protect your own honour and feelings."

This conversation but indicates the tone of many others which occupied the hours mother and son passed together during Sophy's convalescence. And the son, being the weaker character of the two, was insensibly moved and moulded to all Madame's opinions. Indeed, before Sophy was well enough to begin the course of study marked out for her, Archie had become thoroughly convinced that it was his first duty to his wife and himself to insist upon it.

The weak, loving woman made no objections. Indeed, Archie's evident enthusiasm sensibly affected her own desires. She listened with pleasure to the plans for her education, and promised " as soon as she was able, to do her very best."

And there was a strange pathos in the few words " as soon as I am able," which Archie remembered years afterwards, when it was far too late. At the moment, they touched him but lightly; but *Oh, afterwards!* Oh, afterwards! when memory brought back the vision of the small white face on the white pillow, and the faint golden light of the golden curls shadowing the large blue eyes that even then had in them that wide gaze and wistfulness that marks those predestined for sorrow or early death. Alas ! alas ! we see too late, we hear too late, when it is the dead who open the eyes and the ears of the living !

CHAPTER VIII

A GREAT DELIVERANCE

WHILE these clouds of sorrow were slowly gathering in the splendid house of Braelands, there was a full tide of grief and anxiety in the humble cottage of the Binnies. The agony of terror which had changed Janet Binnie's countenance, and sent Christina flying up the cliff for help, was well warranted by Andrew's condition. The man was in the most severe maniacal delirium of brain inflammation, and before the dawning of the next day, required the united strength of two of his mates to control him. To leave her mother and brother in this extremity would have been a cruelty beyond the contemplation of Christina Binnie. Its possibility never entered her mind. All her anger and sense of wrong vanished before the pitiful sight of the strong man in the throes of his mental despair and physical agony. She could not quite ignore her waiting lover, even in such an hour; but she was not a ready writer, so her words were few and to the point: —

DEAR JAMIE, — Andrew is ill, and like to die, and my place, dear lad, is here, until some change come. I must stand by mother and Andrew now, and you yourself would bid me do so. Death is in the house and by the pillow, and there is only God's mercy to trust to. Andrew is clean off his senses, and ill to manage, so you will know that he was not in reason when he spoke so wrong to you, and you will be sorry for him and forgive the words he said, because he did not know what he was saying; and now he knows nothing at all, not even his mother. Do not forget to pray for us in our sorrow, dear Jamie, and I will keep ever a prayer round about you in case of danger on the sea or on land. Your true, troth-plighted wife,

CHRISTINA BINNIE.

This letter was her last selfish act for many a week. After it had been written, she put all her own affairs out of her mind and set herself with heart and soul, by day and by night, to the duty before her. She suffered no shadow of the bygone to darken her calm, strong face, or to weaken the hands and heart from which so much was now expected. And she continually told herself not to doubt in these dark days the mercy of the Eternal, taking hope and comfort, as she went about her duties, from a few words Janet had said, even while she was weeping bitterly over her son's sufferings: —

" But I am putting all fear, Christina, under

my feet; for nothing comes to pass without
helping on some great end."

Now what great end Andrew's severe illness
was to help on, Christina could not divine; but
like her brave mother, she put fear under her
feet, and looked confidently for " the end " which
she trusted would be accomplished in God's
time and mercy.

So week after week the two women walked
with love and courage by the sick man's side,
through the Valley of the Shadow of Death.
Often his life lay but within his lips, and they
watched with prayer continually, lest he should
slip away to them that had gone before,wanting
its mighty shield in the great perilous journey
of the soul. And though there is no open vision in these days, yet His Presence is ever near
to those who seek him with all the heart. So
that wonderful things were seen and experienced
in that humble room, where the man lay at the
point of death.

Andrew had his share of these experiences.
Whatever God said to the waiting, watching
women, He kept for His suffering servant some
of His richest consolations, and so made all his
bed in his sickness. Andrew was keenly sensible of these ministrations, and he grew strong
in their heavenly strength ; for though the vaults
of God are full of wine, the soul that has drunk

of His strong wine of Pain knows that it has tasted the costliest vintage of all, and asks on this earth no better.

And as our thoughts affect our surroundings, quite as much as rain or sunshine affect the atmosphere, these two women, with the sick man on their hearts and hands, were not unhappy women. They did their very best, and trusted God for the outcome. Thus Heaven helped them, and their neighbours helped them, and taking turns in their visitation, they found the Kirk also to be a big, calm friend in the time of their trouble. And then one morning, before the dawn broke, when life seemed to be at its lowest point, when hope was nearly gone, and the shadow of Death fell across the sick man's face, there was suddenly a faint, strange flutter. Some mighty one went out of the door, as the sunshine touched the lintel, and the life began to turn back, just as the tide began to flow.

Then Janet rose up softly and opened the house door, and looking at her son and at the turning waters, she said solemnly: —

" Thank God, Christina! He has turned with the tide? He is all right now."

It was April, however, in its last days, before Andrew had strength sufficient to go down the cliff, and the first news he heard in the village, was that Mistress Braelands had lain at death's door also. Doubtless it explained some testimony private to his own experience, for he let the intelligence pass through his ear-chambers into his heart, without remark, but it made there a great peace — a peace pure and loving as that which passeth understanding.

There was, however, no hope or expectation of his resuming work until the herring fishing in June, and Janet and Christina were now suffering sorely from a strange dilemma. Never before in all their lives had they known what it was to be pinched for ready money. It was hard for Janet to realise that there was no longer "a little bit in the Largo bank to fall back on." Naturally economical, and always regarding it as a sacred duty to live within the rim of their shilling, they had never known either the slow terror of gathering debt, or the acute pinch of actual necessity. But Andrew's long sickness, with all its attendant expenses, had used up all Janet's savings, and the day at last dawned when they must either borrow money or run into debt.

It was a strange and humiliating position, especially after Janet's little motherly bragging about her Christina's silken wedding gown, and brawly furnished floor in Glasgow. Both mother and daughter felt it sorely; and Christina looked at her brother with some little angry

amazement, for he appeared to be quite oblivious
of their cruel strait. He said little about his
work, and never spoke at all about Sophy or
his lost money. In the tremendous furnace of
his affliction, these elements of it appeared to
have been utterly consumed.

Neither mother nor sister liked to remind
him of them, nor yet to point out the poverty
to which his long sickness had reduced them.
It might be six weeks before the herring fishing
roused him to labour, and they had spent their
last sixpence. Janet began seriously to think
of lifting the creel to her shoulders again, and
crying " fresh fish " in Largo streets. It was so
many years since she had done this, that the
idea was painful both to Christina and herself.
The girl would gladly have taken her mother's
place, but this Janet would not hearken to.
As yet, her daughter had never had to haggle
and barter among fish-wives, and house-wives;
and she would not have her do it for a passing
necessity. Besides Jamie might not like it; and
for many other reasons, the little downcome
would press hardest upon Christina.

There was one other plan by which a little
ready money could be raised — that was, to get
a small mortgage on the cottage, and when all
had been said for and against this project, it
seemed, after all, to be the best thing to do.

Griselda Kilgour had money put away, and Christina was very certain she would be glad to help them on such good security as a house and an acre or two of land. Certainly Janet and Griselda had parted in bad bread at their last interview; but in such a time of trouble, Christina did not believe that her kinswoman would remember ill words that had passed, especially as they were about Sophy's marriage — a subject on which they had every right to feel hurt and offended.

Still a mortgage on their home was a dreadful alternative to these simple-minded women; they looked upon it as something very like a disgrace. " A lawyer's foot on the threshold," said Janet, "and who or what is to keep him from putting the key of the cottage in his own pocket, and sending us into a cold and roofless world? No! No! Christina. I had better by far lift the creel to my shoulders again. Thank God, I have the health and strength to do it ! "

" And what will folks be saying of me, to let you ware yourself on the life of that work, in your old age? If you turn fish-wife again, then I be to seek service with some one who can pay me for my hands' work."

" Well, well, my dear lass, to-night we cannot work, but we may sleep; and many a blessing comes, and us not thinking of it. Lie down a wee, and God will comfort you; forbye, the pillow often gives us good counsel. Keep a still heart to-night, and to-morrow is another day."

Janet followed her own advice, and was soon sleeping as soundly and as sweetly as a play-tired child; but Christina sat in the open door-way, thinking of the strait they were in, and wondering if it would not be the kindest and wisest thing to tell Andrew plainly of their necessity. Sooner or later, he would find out that his mother was making his bread for him; and she thought such knowledge, coming from strangers, or through some accident, would wound him more severely than if she herself explained their hard position to him. As for the mortgage, the very thought of it made her sick. "It is just giving our home away, bit by bit — that is what a mortgage is — and whatever we are to do, and whatever I ought to do, God only knows!"

Yet in spite of the stress of this, to her, terrible question, a singular serenity possessed her. It was as if she had heard a voice saying "Peace, be still!" She thought it was the calm of nature, — the high tide breaking gently on the shingle with a low murmur, the soft warmth, the full moonshine, the sound of the fisher-men's voices calling faintly on the horizon, —

and still more, the sense of divine care and knowledge, and the sweet conviction that One, mighty to help and to save, was her Father and her Friend. For a little space she walked abreast of angels. So many things take place in the soul that are not revealed, and it is always when we are wrestling *alone*, that the comforting ones come. Christina looked downward to the village sleeping at her feet,

> " Beneath its little patch of sky,
> And little lot of stars,"

and upward, to where innumerable worlds were whirling noiselessly through the limitless void, and forgot her own clamorous personality and " the something that infects the world; " and doing this, though she did not voice her anxiety, it passed from her heart into the Infinite Heart, and thus she was calmed and comforted. Then, suddenly, the prayer of her childhood and her girlhood came to her lips, and she stood up, and clasping her hands, she cast her eyes towards heaven, and said reverently : —

> " *This is the change of Thy Right Hand, O Thou Most*
> *High !*
> *Thou art strong to strengthen !*
> *Thou art gracious to help !*
> *Thou art ready to better !*
> *Thou art mighty to save !* "

As the words passed her lips, she heard a movement, and softly and silently as a spirit, her brother Andrew, fully dressed, passed through the door-way. His arm lightly touched Christina's clothing, but he was unconscious of her presence. He looked more than mortal, and was evidently seeing *through* his eyes, and not *with* them. She was afraid to speak to him. She did not dream of touching him, or of arresting his steps. Without a sign or word, he went rapidly down the cliff, walking with that indifference to physical obstacles which a spirit that had cast off its incarnation might manifest.

" He is walking in his sleep, and he may get into danger or find death itself," thought Christina, and her fear gave strength and fleet-ness to her footsteps as she quickly followed her brother. He made no noise of any kind; he did not even disturb a pebble in his path; but went forward, with a motion light and rapid, and the very reverse of the slow, heavy-footed gait of a fisherman. But she kept him in sight as he glided over the ribbed and water-lined sands, and rounded the rocky points which jutted into the sea water. After a walk of nearly two miles, he made direct for a series of bold rocks which were penetrated by number-less caverns, and into one of these he entered.

Hitherto he had not shown a moment's

hesitation; nor did he now, though the path was dangerously narrow and rocky, overhanging unfathomable abysses of dark water. But Christina was in mortal terror, both for herself and Andrew. She did not dare to call his name, lest, in the sudden awakening, he might miss his precarious foothold, and fall to unavoidable death. She found it almost impossible to follow him; nor indeed in her ordinary frame of mind could she have done so. But the experience, so strange and thrilling, had lifted her in a measure above the control of the physical, and she was conscious of an exaltation of spirit which defied difficulties that would ordinarily have terrified her. Still she was so much delayed by the precautions evidently necessary for her life, that she lost sight of her brother, and her heart stood still with fright.

Prayers parted her white lips continually, as she slowly climbed the hollow crags that seemed to close together and forbid her further progress. But she would not turn back, for she could not believe that Andrew had perished. She would have heard the fall of his body or its splash in the water beneath, and so she continued to climb and clamber, though every step appeared to make further exploration more and more impossible.

With a startling unexpectedness, she found herself in a circular chamber, open to the sky, and on one of the large boulders lying around, Andrew sat. He was still in the depths of a somnambulistic sleep; but he had his lost box of gold and bank-notes before him, and he was counting the money. She held her breath. She stood still as a stone. She was afraid to think. But she divined at once the whole secret. Motionless she watched him, as he unrolled and rerolled the notes, as he counted and recounted the gold, and then carefully locked the box, and hid the key under the edge of the stone on which he sat.

What would he now do with the box? She watched his movements with a breathless interest. He sat still for a few moments, clasping his treasure firmly in his large, brown hands; then he rose, and put it in an aperture above his head, filling the space in front of it with a stone that exactly fitted. Without hurry, and without hesitation, the whole transaction was accomplished; and then, with an equal composure and confidence, he retraced his steps through the cavern and over the rocks and sands to his own sleeping room.

Christina followed as rapidly as she was able; but her exaltation had died away, and left her weak and ready to weep; so that when she reached the open beach, Andrew was so far in advance as to be almost out of sight. She could not hope to overtake him, and she sat down for a few minutes to try and realise' the great relief that had come to them — to wonder — to clasp her hands in adoration, to weep tears of joy. When she reached her home at last, it was quite light. She looked into her brother's room, and saw that he was lying motionless in the deepest sleep; but Janet was half-awake, and she asked sleepily : —

" Whatever are you about so early for, Christina? Is n't the day long enough for the sorrow and the care of it ? "

" Oh, Mother! Mother! The day is n't long enough for the joy and the blessing of it."

" What do you mean, my lass? What is it in your face? What have you seen? Who has spoken a word to you?" and Janet rose up quickly, and put her hands on Christina's shoulders; for the girl was swaying and trembling, and ready to break out into a passion of sobbing.

" I have seen, Mother, the salvation of the Lord! I have found Andrew's lost money! I have proved that poor Jamie is innocent! We arena poor any longer. There is no need to borrow, or mortgage, or to run in debt. Oh, Mother! Mother! The blessing you bespoke last night, the blessing we were not thinking of, has come to us."

"The Lord be thanked! I knew He would save us, in His own time, and His time is never too late."

Then Christina sat down by her mother's side, and in low, intense tones, told her all she had seen. Janet listened with kindling face and shining eyes.

"The mercy of God is on His beloved, and His regard is unto His elect," she cried, "and I am glad this day, that I never doubted Him, and never prayed to Him with a grudge at the bottom of my heart." Then she began to dress herself with her old joyfulness, humming a line of this and that psalm or paraphrase, and stopping in the middle to ask Christina another question; until the kettle began to simmer to her happy mood, and she suddenly sung out joyfully four lines, never very far from her lips: —

> "My heart is dashed with cares and fears,
>   My song comes fluttering and is gone;
>   Oh! high above this home of tears,
>   Eternal Joy sing on!"

How would it feel for the hyssop on the wall to turn cedar, I wonder? Just about as Janet and Christina felt that morning, eating their simple breakfast with glad hearts. Poor as the viands were, they had the flavour of joy and thankfulness, and of a wondrous salvation. "It is the Lord's doing!" This was the key to which the two women set all their hopes and rejoicing, and yet even into its noble melody there stole at last a little of the fret of earth. For suddenly Janet had a fear — not of God, but of man — and she said anxiously to her daughter : —

" You should have brought the box home with you, Christina. O my lass, if some other body should have seen what you have seen, then we will be fairly ruined twice over."

" No, no, Mother! I would not have touched the box for all there is in it. Andrew must go for it himself. He might never believe it was where I saw it, if he did not go for it. You know well he suspicioned both Jamie and me; and indeed, Mother dear, you yourself thought worse of Jamie than you should have done."

" Let that be now, Christina. God has righted all. We will have no casts-up. If I thought of any one wrongly, I am sorry for it, and I could not say more than that even to my Maker. If ill news was waiting for Andrew, it would have shaken him off his pillow ere this."

" Let him sleep. His soul took his body a weary walk this morning. He is sore needing sleep, no doubt."

" He will have to wake up now, and go about his business. It is high time."

"You should mind, Mother, what a tempest he has come through; all the waves and billows of sorrow have gone over him."

"He is a good man, and ought to be the better of the tempest. His ship may have been sorely beaten and tossed, but his anchor was fast all through the storm. It is time he lifted anchor now, and faced the brunt and the buffet again. An idle man, if he is not a sick man, is on a lee shore; let him put out to sea; why, lassie! a storm is better than a shipwreck."

" To be sure, Mother. Here the dear lad comes ! " and with that Andrew sauntered slowly into the kitchen. There was no light on his face, no hope or purpose in his movements. He sat down at the table, and drew his cup of tea towards him with an air of indifference, almost of despair. It wounded Janet. She put her hand on his hand, and compelled him to look into her face. As he did so, his eyes opened wide; speculation, wonder, something like hope came into them. The very silence of the two women — a silence full of meaning — arrested his soul. He looked from one to the other, and saw the same inscrutable joy answering his gaze.

"What is it, Mother?" he asked. "I can see you have something to tell me."

"I have that, Andrew! O my dear lad, your money is found! I do not think a penny-bit of it is missing. Don't mind me! I am greeting for the very joy of it — but O Andrew, you be to praise God! It is his doing, and marvellous in our eyes. Ask Christina. She can tell you better than I can."

But Andrew could not speak. He touched his sister's hand, and dumbly looked into her happy face. He was white as death, but he sat bending forward to her, with one hand outstretched, as if to clasp and grasp the thing she had to tell him. So Christina told him the whole story, and after he had heard it, he pushed his plate and cup away, and rose up, and went into his room and shut the door. And Janet said gratefully: —

"It is all right, Christina. He'll get nothing but good advice in God's council chamber. We'll not need to worry ourselves again anent either the lad or the money. The one has come to his senses, and the other will come to its use. And we will cast nothing up to him; the best boat loses her rudder once in a while."

It was not long before Andrew joined his mother and sister, and the man was a changed man. There was grave purpose in his calm

183

face, and a joy, too deep for words, in the glint of his eyes and in the graciousness of his manner.

"Come, Christina!" he said. "I want you you to go with me; we will bring the siller home together. But I forget — it is maybe too far for you to walk again to-day?"

"I would walk ten times as far to pleasure you, Andrew. Do you know the place I told you of?"

"Aye, I know it well. I hid the first few shillings there that I ever saved."

As they walked together over the sands Christina said: "I wonder, Andrew, when and how you carried the box there? Can you guess at all the way this trouble came about?"

"I can; but I'm ashamed to tell you, Christina. You see, after I had shown you the money, I took a fear anent it. I thought maybe you might tell Jamie Logan, and the possibility of this fretted on my mind until it became a sure thing with me. So, being troubled in my heart, I doubtless got up in my sleep and put the box in my oldest and safest hiding-place."

"But why then did you not remember that you had done so?"

"You see, dearie, I hid it in my sleep, so then it was only in my sleep I knew where I had put it. There is two of us, I am thinking, lassie, and the one man does not always tell the other man all he knows. I ought to have trusted you, Christina; but I doubted you, and, as mother says, doubt aye fathers sin or sorrow of some kind or other."

"You might have safely trusted me, Andrew."

"I know now I might. But he is lifeless that is faultless; and the wrong I have done I must put right. I am thinking of Jamie Logan?"

"Poor Jamie! You know now that he never wronged you?"

"I know, and I will let him know as soon as possible. When did you hear from him? And where is he at all?"

"I don't know just where he is. He sailed away yon time; and when he got to New York, he left the ship."

"What for did he do that?"

"O Andrew, I cannot tell. He was angry with me for not coming to Glasgow as I promised him I would."

"You promised him that?"

"Aye, the night you were taken so bad. But how could I leave you in Dead Man's Dale? and mother here lone to help you through it. So I wrote and told him I be to see you through your trouble, and he went away from Scotland and said he would never come back again till we found out how sorely all of us had wronged him."

"Don't cry, Christina! I will seek Jamie over the wide world till I find him. I wonder at myself. I am shamed of myself. However, will you forgive me for all the sorrow I have brought on you?"

"You were not altogether to blame, Andrew. You were ill to death at the time. Your brain was on fire, poor laddie, and it would be a sin to hold you countable for any word you said or did not say. But if you will seek after Jamie, either by letter or your own travel, and say as much to him as you have said to me, I may be happy yet, for all that has come and gone."

"What else can I do but seek the lad I have wronged so cruelly? What else can I do for the sister that never deserved ill word or deed from me? No, I cannot rest until I have made the wrong to both of you as far right as sorrow and siller can do."

When they reached the cavern, Andrew would not let Christina enter it with him. He said he knew perfectly well the spot to which he must go, and he would not have her tread again the dangerous road. So Christina sat down on the rocks to wait for him, and the water tinkled beneath her feet, and the sunshine dimpled the water, and the fresh salt wind blew strength and happiness into her heart and hopes. In a short

time, the last moment of her anxiety was over;
and Andrew came back to her, with the box
and its precious contents in his hands. " It
is all here ! " he said, and his voice had its old
tones; for his heart was ringing to the music
of its happiness, knowing that the door of
fortune was now open to him, and that he
could walk up to success, as to a friend, on
his own hearthstone.

That afternoon he put the money in Largo
bank, and made arrangements for his mother's
and sister's comfort for some weeks. "For
there is nothing I can do for my own side, until
I have found Jamie Logan, and put Christina's
and his affairs right," he said. And Janet was of
the same opinion.

" You cannot bless yourself, laddie, until you
bless others," she said, " and the sooner you go
about the business, the better for everybody."

So that night Andrew started for Glasgow,
and when he reached that city, he was fortunate enough to find the very ship in which
Jamie had sailed away, lying at her dock. The
first mate recalled the young man readily.

" The more by token that he had my own
name," he said to Andrew. " We are both of
us Fife Logans, and I took a liking to the lad,
and he told me his trouble."

" About some lost money? " asked Andrew.

" Nay, he said nothing about money. It was some love trouble, I take it. He thought he could better forget the girl if he ran away from his country and his work. He has found out his mistake by this time, no doubt."

" You knew he was going to leave ' The Line ' then? "

" Yes, we let him go; and I heard say that he had shipped on an American line, sailing to Cuba, or New Orleans, or somewhere near the equator."

" Well, I shall try and find him."

" I wouldn't, if I was you. He is sure to come back to his home again. He showed me a lock of the lassie's hair. Man! a single strand of it would pull him back to Scotland sooner or later."

" But I have wronged him sorely. I did not mean to wrong him, but that does not alter the case."

" Not a bit. Love sickness is one thing; a wrong against a man's good name or good fortune, is a different matter. I would find him and right him."

" That is what I want to do."

And so when the *Circassia* sailed out of Greenock for New York, Andrew Binnie sailed in her. " It is not a very convenient journey," he said rather sadly, as he left Scotland behind him; "but wrong has been done, and wrong has no warrant, and I'll never have a good day till I put the wrong right; so the sooner the better, for, as Mother says, 'that which a fool does at the end a wise man does at the beginning.'"

CHAPTER IX

THE RIGHTING OF A WRONG

So Andrew sailed for New York, and life resumed its long forgotten happy tenor in the Binnie cottage. Janet sang about her spotless houseplace, feeling almost as if it was a new gift of God to her; and Christina regarded their small and simple belongings with that tender and excessive affection which we are apt to give to whatever has been all but lost and then unexpectedly recovered. Both women involuntarily showed this feeling in the extra care they took of everything. Never had the floors and chairs and tables been scrubbed and rubbed to such spotless beauty; and every cup and platter and small ornament was washed and dusted with such care as could only spring from heart-felt gratitude in its possession. Naturally they had much spare time; for, as Janet said, "having no man to cook and wash for lifted half the work from their hands;" but they were busy women for all that. Janet began a patch-work quilt of a wonderful design as a wedding present for Christina; and as the whole village contributed "pieces" for its construction, the whole village felt an interest in its progress. It was a delightful excuse for Janet's resumption of her old friendly, gossipy ways; and every afternoon saw her in some crony's house, spreading out her work, and explaining her design, and receiving the praises and sometimes the advice of her acquaintances.

Christina also, quietly but yet hopefully, began again her preparations for her marriage; for Janet laughed at her fears and doubts. "Andrew was sure to find Jamie, and Jamie was sure to be glad to come home again. It stands to reason," she said confidently. "The very sight of Andrew will be a cordial of gladness to him; for he will know, as soon as he sees the face of him, that the brother will mean the sister and the wedding ring. If you get the spindle and distaff ready, my lass, God is sure to send the flax; and by the same token, if you get your plenishing made and marked, and your bride-clothes finished, God will certainly send the husband."

"Jamie said in his last letter — the one in which he bid me farewell — 'I will never come back to Scotland.'"

"*Toots! Havers!* 'I *will*' is for the Lord God Almighty to say. A sailor-man's 'I will' is just breath, that any wind may blow away. When Andrew gives him the letter you sent, Jamie will not be able to wait for the next boat for Scotland."

"He may have taken a fancy to America and want to stop there."

"What are you talking about, Christina Binnie? There is nothing but scant and want in them foreign countries. Oh! my lass, he will come home, and be glad to come home; and you will have the hank in your own hand. See that you spin it cannily and happily."

"I hope Andrew will not make himself sick again looking for the lost."

"I shall have little pity for him, if he does. I told him to make good days for himself; why not? He is about his duty; the law of kindness is in his heart, and the purpose of putting right what he put wrong is the wind that drives him. Well then, his journey — be it short or long — ought to be a holiday to him; and a body does not deserve a holiday if he cannot take advantage of one. Them were my last words to Andrew."

"Jamie may have seen another lass. I have heard say the lassies in America are gey bonnie."

"I'll just be stepping if you have nothing but frets and fears to say. When things go wrong, it is mostly because folks will have them wrong and no other way."

"In this world, Mother, the giffs and the gaffs — "

"In this world, Christina, the giffs and the gaffs generally balance one another. And if they don't, — mind what I say, — it is because there is a moral defect on the failing side. Oh! but women are flightersome and easy frighted."

"Whyles you have fears yourself, Mother."

"Ay, I am that foolish whyles; but I shall be a sick, weak body, when I can't outmarch the worst of them."

"You are just an oracle, Mother."

"Not I; but if I was a very saint, I would say every morning of my life: 'Now then, Soul, hope for good and have good.' Many a sad heart folks get they have no need to have. Take out your needle and thimble and go to your wedding clothes, lassie; you will need them before the summer is over. You may take my word for that."

"If Jamie should still love me."

"Love you! He will be that far gone in love with you that there will be no help for him but standing up before the minister. That will be seen and heard tell of. Lift your white seam, and be busy at it; there is noth-

ing else to do till tea time, and I am away for
an hour or two to Maggie Buchans. Her man
went to Edinburgh this morning. What for,
I don't know yet, but I'll maybe find out."

It was on this very afternoon that Janet first
heard that there was trouble and a sound of
more trouble at Braelands. Sophy had driven
down in her carriage the previous day to see her
cousin Isobel Murray, and some old friends
who had gone into Isobel's had found the
little Mistress of Braelands weeping bitterly
in her cousin's arms. After this news, Janet
did not stay long at Maggie Buchans; she
carried her patch-work to Isobel Murray's, and
as Isobel did not voluntarily name the subject,
Janet boldly introduced it herself.

"I heard tell that Sophy Braelands was here
yesterday."

"Aye, she was."

"A grand thing for you, Isobel, to have the
Braelands's yellow coach and pair standing
before the Murray cottage all of two or three
hours."

"It did not stand before my cottage, Janet.
The man went to the public house and gave
the horses a drink, and himself one too, or I
am much mista'en, for I had to send little
Pete Galloway after him."

"I think Sophy might have called on me."

"No doubt she would have done so, had she known that Andrew was away; but I never thought to tell her until the last moment."

"Is she well? I was hearing that she looked but poorly."

"You were hearing the truth. She looks bad enough."

"Is she happy, Isobel?"

"I never asked her that question."

"You have eyes and observation. Did n't you ask yourself that question?"

"Maybe I did."

"What then?"

"I have nothing to say anent it."

"What was she talking about? You know, Isobel, that Sophy is kin of mine, and I loved her mother like my own sister. So I be to feel anxious about the little body. I 'm feared things are not going as well as they might do. Madame Braelands is but a hard-grained woman."

"She is as cruel a woman and as bad a woman as there is between this and wherever she may be."

"Is n't she at Braelands?"

"Not for a week or two. She 's away to Acker Castle, and her son with her."

"And why not Sophy also?"

"The poor lassie would not go — she says she

could not. Well, Janet, I may as good confess that there is something wrong that she does not like to speak of yet. She is just at the crying-point now; the reason why and wherefore will come anon."

"But she be to say something to you."

"I 'll tell you. She said she was worn out with learning this and that, and she was humbled to death to find out how ignorant and full of faults she was. Madame Braclands is both schoolmistress and mother-in-law, and there does not seem to be a minute of the day in which the poor child is n't checked and corrected. She has lost all her pretty ways, and she says she cannot learn Madame's ways; and she is feared for herself, and shamed for herself. And when the invitation came for Acker Castle, Madame told her she must not accept it for her husband's sake, because all his great friends were to be there, and they were to discuss his going to Parliament, and she would only shame and disgrace him. And you may well conceive that Sophy turned obstinate and said she would bide in her own home. And, someway, her husband did not urge her to go, and this hurt her worst of all; and she felt lonely and broken-hearted, and so came to see me. That is everything about it; but keep it to yourself, Janet, it is n't for common clash."

196

"I know that. But did Madame Braelands and her son really go away and leave Sophy her lone?"

"They left her with two or three teachers to worry the life out of her. They went away two days ago; and Madame was in full feather and glory, with her son at her beck and call, and all her grand airs and manners about her. Sophy says she watched them away from her bedroom window, and then she cried her heart out. And she could n't learn her lessons, and so sent the man teacher and the woman teacher about their business. She says she will not try the weary books again to please anybody; they make her head ache so that she is like to swoon away."

"Sophy was never fond of books; but I thought she would like the music."

"Aye, if they would let her have her own way about it. She has her father's little fiddle, and when she was but a bare-footed lassie, she played on it wonderful."

"I remember. You would have thought there was a linnet living inside of it."

"Well, she wanted to have some lessons on it, and her husband was willing enough, but Madame went into hysterics about the idea of anything so vulgar. There is a constant bitter little quarrel between the two women, and

Sophy says she cannot go to her husband with every slight and cruelty. Madame laughs at her, or pretends to pet her, or else gets into passions at what she calls Sophy's unreasonableness; and Archie Braelands is weary to death of complaining, and just turns sulky or goes out of the house. Oh, Janet, I can see and feel the bitter, cruel task-woman over the poor, foolish child! She is killing her, and Archie Braelands does not see the right and the wrong of it all."

"I 'll make him see it."

"You will hold your tongue, Janet. They who stir in muddy water only make it worse."

"But Archie Braelands loved her, or he would not have married her; and if he knew the right and the wrong of poor Sophy's position — "

"I tell you, that is nothing to it, Janet."

"It is everything to it. Right is right, in the devil's teeth."

"I 'm sorry I said a word to you; it is a dangerous thing to get between a man and his wife. I would not do it, not even for Sophy; for reason here or reason there, folks be to take care of themselves; and my man gets siller from Braelands, more than we can afford to lose."

"You are taken with a fit of the prudentials,

Isobel; and it is just extraordinar' how selfish they make folk."

And yet Janet herself, when going over the conversation with Christina, was quite inclined on second thoughts not to interfere in Sophy's affairs, though both were anxious and sorrowful about the motherless little woman.

"She ought to be with her husband wherever he is, court or castle," said Christina. "She is a foolish woman to let him go away with her enemy, and such a clever enemy as Madame Braelands is. I think, Mother, you ought to call on Sophy, and give her a word of love and a bit of good advice. Her mother was very close to you."

"I know, Christina; but Isobel was right about the folly of coming between a man and his wife. I would just get the wyte of it. Many a sore heart I have had for meddling with what I could not mend."

Yet Janet carried the lonely, sorrowful little wife on her heart continually; though, after a week or two had passed and nothing new was heard from Braelands, every one began to give their sympathy to Christina and her affairs. Janet was ready to talk of them. There were some things she wished to explain, though she was too proud to do so until her friends felt interest enough to ask for explanations. And as soon as it was discovered that Andrew had gone to America, the interest and curiosity was sufficiently keen and eager to satisfy even Janet.

"It fairly took the breath from me," said Sabrina Roy, "when I was told the like of that. I cannot think there is a word of truth in such a report."

Mistress Roy was sitting at Janet's fireside, and so had the privilege of a guest; but, apart from this, it gave Janet a profound satisfaction to answer: "Ay, well, Sabrina, the clash is true for once in a lifetime. Andrew has gone to America, and the Lord knows where else beside."

"Preserve us all! I would n't believe it, only from your own lips, Janet. Whatever would be the matter that sent him stravaging round the world, with no ship of his own beneath his feet or above his head?"

"A matter of right and wrong, Sabrina. My Andrew has a strict conscience and a sense of right that would be ornamental in a very saint. Not to make a long story of it, he and Jamie Logan had a quarrel. It was the night Andrew took his inflammation, and it is very sure his brain was on fire and off its judgment at the time. But we were none of us thinking of the like of that; and so the bad words came, and stirred up the bad blood, and if I had n't been there myself, there might have been spilled blood to end all with, for they were both black angry."

"Guide us, woman! What was it all about?"

. "Well, Sabrina, it was about siller; that is all I am free to say. Andrew was sure he was right, and Jamie was sure he was wrong; and they were going fairly to one another's throats, when I stepped in and flung them apart."

"And poor Christina had the buff and the buffet to take and to bear for their tempers?"

"Not just that. Jamie begged her to go away with him, and the lassie would have gone if I had n't got between her and the door. I had a hard few minutes, I can tell you, Sabrina; for when men are beside themselves with passion, they are in the devil's employ, and it 's no easy work to take a job out of *his* hands. But I sent Jamie flying down the cliff, and I locked the door and put the key in my pocket, and ordered Andrew and Christina off to their beds, and thought I would leave the rest of the business till the next day; but before midnight Andrew was raving, and the affair was out of my hands altogether."

"It is a wonder Christina did not go after her lad."

"What are you talking about, Sabrina? It

would have been a world's wonder and a black, burning shame if my girl had gone after her lad in such a calamitous time. No, no, Christina Binnie is n't the kind of girl that shrinks in the wetting. When her time of trial came, she did the whole of her duty, showing herself day by day a witness and a testimony to her decent, kirk-going forefathers."

"And so Andrew has found out he was wrong and Jamie Logan right?"

"Aye, he has. And the very minute he did so, he made up his mind to seek the lad far and near and confess his fault."

"And bring him back to Christina?"

"Just so. What for not? He parted them, and he has the right and duty to bring them together again, though it take the best years of his life and the last bawbee of his money."

"Folks were saying his money was all spent."

"Folks are far wrong then. Andrew has all the money he ever had. Andrew is n't a bragger, and his money has been silent so far, but it will speak ere long."

"With money to the fore, you should n't have been so scrimpit with yourselves in such a time of work and trouble. Folks noticed it."

"I don't believe in wasting anything, Sabrina, even grief. I did not spend a penny, nor a tear, nor a bit of strength, that was useless.

What for should I? And if folks noticed we were scrimpit, why did n't they think about helping us? No, thank God! We have enough and a good bit to spare, for all that has come and gone, and if it pleases the Maker of Happiness to bring Jamie Logan back again, we will have a bridal that will make a monumental year in Pittendurie."

"I am glad to hear tell o' that. I never did approve of two or three at a wedding. The more the merrier."

"That is a very sound observe. My Christina will have a wedding to be seen and heard tell of from one sacramental occasion to another."

"Well, then, good luck to Andrew Binnie, and may he come soon home and well home, and sorrow of all kinds keep a day's sail behind him. And surely he will go back to the boats when he has saved his conscience, for there is never a better sailor and fisher on the North Sea. The men were all saying that when he was so ill."

"It is the very truth. Andrew can read the sea as well as the minister can read the Book. He never turns his back on it; his boat is always ready to kiss the wind in its teeth. I have been with him when *rip! rip! rip!* went her canvas; but I had n't a single fear, I knew the lad at the helm. I knew he would bring her to her bearings beautifully. He always did; and then how the gallant bit of a creature would shake herself and away like a sea-gull. My Andrew is a son of the sea as all his forbears were. Its salt is in his blood, and when the tide is going with a race and a roar, and the break of the waves and the howl of the wind is like a thousand guns, then Andrew Binnie is in the element he likes best; aye, though his boat be spinning round like a laddie's top."

"Well, Janet, I will be going."

"Mind this, Sabrina, I have told you all to my heart's keel; and if folks are saying to you that Jamie has given Christina the slip, or that the Binnies are scrimpit for poverty's sake, or the like of any other ill-natured thing, you will be knowing how to answer them."

"'Deed, I will! And I am real glad things are so well with you all, Janet."

"Well, and like to be better, thank God, as soon as Andrew gets back from foreign parts."

In the meantime, Andrew, after a pleasant sail, had reached New York. He made many friends on the ship, and in the few days of bad weather usually encountered came to the front, as he always did when winds were blowing and sailor-men had to wear oil skins. The first sight of the New World made him silent.

He was too prudent to hazard an opinion about any place so remote and so strange, though he cautiously admitted "the lift was as blue as in Scotland and the sunshine not to speak ill of." But as his ideas of large towns had been formed upon Edinburgh and Glasgow, he could hardly admire New York. "It looks," he said to an acquaintance who was showing him the city, "it looks as if it had been built in a hurry;" for he was thinking of the granite streets and piers of Glasgow. "Besides," he added, "there is no romance or beauty about it; it is all straight lines and squares. Man alive! you should see Edinburgh the sel' of it, the castle, and the links, and the bonnie terraces, and the Highland men parading the streets; it is just a bit of poetry made out of builders' stones."

With the information he had received from the mate of the "Circassia," and his advice and directions, Andrew had little difficulty in locating Jamie Logan. He found his name in the list of seamen sailing a steamer between New York and New Orleans; and this steamer was then lying at her pier on the North River. It was not very hard to obtain permission to interview Jamie; and armed with this authority, he went to the ship one very hot afternoon about four o'clock.

Jamie was at the hold, attending to the un-shipping of cargo; and as he lifted himself from the stooping attitude which his work demanded, he saw Andrew Binnie approaching him. He pretended, however, not to see him, and became suddenly very deeply interested in the removal of a certain case of goods. Andrew was quite conscious of the affectation, but he did not blame Jamie; it only made him the more anxious to atone for the wrong he had done. He stepped rapidly forward, and with extended hands said: —

"Jamie Logan, I have come all the way from Scotland to ask you to forgive me. I thought wrong of you, and I said wrong to you, and I am sorry for it. Can you pass it by for Christ's sake?"

Jamie looked into the speaker's face, frankly and gravely, but with the air of a man who has found something he thought lost. He took Andrew's hands in his own hands and answered: —

"Aye, I can forgive you with all my heart. I knew you would come to yourself some day, Andrew; but it has seemed a long time wait-ing. I have not a word against you now. A man that can come three thousand miles to own up to a wrong is worth forgiving. How is Christina?"

"Christina is well, but tired-like with the care of me through my long sickness. She has sent you a letter, and here it is. The poor lass has suffered more than either of us; but never a word of complaining from her. Jamie, I have promised her to bring you back with me. Can you come?"

"I will go back to Scotland with you gladly, if it can be managed. I am fair sick for the soft gray skies, and the keen, salt wind of the North Sea. Last Sabbath Day I was in New Orleans — fairly baking with the heat of the place — and I thought I heard the kirk bells across the sands, and saw Christina stepping down the cliff with the Book in her hands and her sweet smile making all hearts but mine happy. Andrew man, I could not keep the tears out of my een, and my heart was away down to my feet, and I was fairly sick with longing."

They left the ship together and spent the night in each other's company. Their room was a small one, in a small river-side hotel, hot and close smelling; but the two men created their own atmosphere. For as they talked of their old life, the clean, sharp breezes of Pittendurie swept through the stifling room; they tasted the brine on the wind's wings, and felt the wet, firm sands under their feet. Or they talked of the fishing-boats, until they could see their sails bellying out, as they lay down just enough to show they felt the fresh wind tossing the spray from their bows and lifting themselves over the great waves as if they stepped over them.

Before they slept, they had talked themselves into a fever of home-sickness, and the first work of the next day was to make arrangements for Jamie's release from his obligations. There was some delay and difficulty about this matter; but it was finally completed to the satisfaction of all parties, and Andrew and Jamie took the next Anchor Line steamer for Glasgow.

On the voyage home, the two men got very close to each other, not in any accidental mood of confidence, but out of a thoughtful and assured conviction of respect. Andrew told Jamie all about his lost money and the plans for his future which had been dependent on it, and Jamie said: —

"No wonder you went off your health and senses with the thought of your loss, Andrew. I would have been less sensible than you. It was an awful experience, man; I cannot tell how you tholed it at all."

"Well, I didn't thole it, Jamie. I just broke down under it, and God Almighty and my mother and sister had to carry me through the ill time; but all is right now. I shall have the boat I was promised, and at the long last be Captain Binnie of the Red-White Fleet. And what for should n't you take a berth with me? I shall have the choosing of my officers, and we will strike hands together, if you like it, and you shall be my second mate to start with."

"I should like nothing better than to sail with you and under you, Andrew. I could n't find a captain more to my liking."

"Nor I, a better second mate. We both know our business, and we shall manage it cleverly and brotherly."

So Jamie's future was settled before the men reached Pittendurie, and the new arrangement well talked over, and Andrew and his proposed brother-in-law were finger and thumb about it. This was a good thing for Andrew, for his secretive, self-contained disposition was his weak point, and had been the cause of all his sorrow and loss of time and suffering.

They had written a letter in New York and posted it the day they left, advising Janet and Christina of the happy home-coming; but both men forgot, or else did not know, that the letter came on the very same ship with themselves, and might therefore or might not reach

home before them. It depended entirely on
the postal authority in Pittendurie. If she
happened to be in a mood to sort the letters as
soon as they arrived, and then if she happened
to see any one passing who could carry a letter
to Janet Binnie, the chances were that Janet
would receive the intelligence of her son's
arrival in time to make some preparation for it.

As it happened, these favourable circumstances occurred, and about four o'clock one
afternoon, as Janet was returning up the cliff
from Isobel Murray's, she met little Tim
Galloway with the letter in his hand.

"It is from America," said the laddie, "and
my mother told me to hurry myself with it.
Maybe there is folk coming after it."

"I'll give you a bawbee for the sense of
your words, Tim," answered Janet; and she
hastened herself and flung the letter into
Christina's lap, saying:—

"Open it, lassie, it will be full of good
news. I shouldn't wonder if both lads were
on their way home again."

"Mother, Mother, they *are* home; they will
be here anon, they will be here this very
night. Oh, Mother, I must put on my best
gown and my gold ear-rings and brush my
hair, and you'll be setting forward the tea
and making a white pudding; for Jamie, you

know, was always saying none but you could mix the meal and salt and pepper, and toast it as it should be done."

"I shall look after the men's eating, Christina, and you make yourself as braw as you like to. Jamie has been long away, and he must have a full welcome home again."

They were both as excited as two happy children; perhaps Janet was most evidently so, for she had never lost her child-heart, and everything pleasant that happened was a joy and a wonder to her. She took out her best damask table-cloth, and opened her bride chest for the real china kept there so carefully; and she made the white pudding with her own hands, and ran down the cliff for fresh fish and the lamb chops which were Andrew's special luxury. And Christina made the curds and cream, and swept the hearth, and set the door wide open for the home-comers.

And as good fortune comes where it is looked for, Andrew and Jamie entered the cottage just as everything was ready for them. There was no waiting, no cooled welcome, no spoiled dainties, no disappointment of any kind. Life was taken up where it had been most pleasantly dropped; all the interval of doubt and suffering was put out of remembrance, and when the joyful meal had been eaten, as Janet washed her cups and saucers and tidied her house, they talked of the happy future before them.

"And I 'll tell you what, bairnies," said the dear old woman as she stood folding her real china in the tissue paper devoted to that purpose, "I 'll tell you what, bairnies, good will asks for good deeds, and I 'll show my good will by giving Christina the acre of land next my own. If Jamie is to go with you, Andrew, and your home is to be with me, lad — "

"Where else would it be, Mother?"

"Well, then, where else need Jamie's home be but in Pittenduric? I 'll give the land for his house, and what will you do, Andrew? Speak for your best self, my lad."

"I will give my sister Christina one hundred gold sovereigns and the silk wedding-gown I promised her."

"Oh, Andrew, my dear brother, how will I ever thank you as I ought to?"

"I owe you more, Christina, than I can count."

"No, no, Andrew," said Janet. "What has Christina done that siller can pay for? You can't buy love with money, and gold is n't in exchange for it. Your gift is a good-will gift. It is n't a paid debt, God be thanked!"

The very next day the little family went

into Largo, and the acre was legally trans-
ferred, and Jamie made arrangements for the
building of his cottage. But the marriage did
not wait on the building; it was delayed no
longer than was necessary for the making of
the silk wedding-gown. This office Griselda
Kilgour undertook with much readiness and an
entire oblivion of Janet's unadvised allusions
to her age. And more than this, Griselda
dressed the bride with her own hands, adding
to her costume a bonnet of white tulle and
orange blossoms that was the admiration of
the whole village, and which certainly had a
bewitching effect above Christina's waving
black hair, and shining eyes, and marvellous
colouring.

And, as Janet desired, the wedding was a
holiday for the whole of Pittendurie. Old
and young were bid to it, and for two days the
dance, the feast, and the song went gayly on;
and for two days not a single fishing-boat left
the little port of Pittendurie. Then the men
went out to sea again, and the women paid
their bride visits, and the children finished all
the dainties that were else like to be wasted,
and life gradually settled back into its usual
grooves.

But though Jamie went to the fishing, pend-
ing Andrew's appointment to his steamboat,

Janet and Christina had a never-ceasing interest in the building and plenishing of Christina's new home. It was not fashionable, nor indeed hardly permissible, for any one to build a house on a plan grander than the traditional fisher cottage; but Christina's, though no larger than her neighbours', had the modern convenience of many little closets and presses, and these Janet filled with homespun napery, linseys, and patchwork, so that never a young lass in Pittendurie began life under such full and happy circumstances.

In the fall of the year the new fire was lit on the new hearth, and Christina moved into her own home. It was only divided from her mother's by a strip of garden and a low fence, and the two women could stand in their open doors and talk to each other. And during the summer all had gone well. Jamie had been fortunate and made money, and Andrew had perfected all his arrangements, so that one morning in early September, the whole village saw "The Falcon" come to anchor in the bay, and Captain Binnie, in his gold-buttoned coat and gold-banded cap, take his place on her bridge, with Jamie, less conspicuously attired, attending him.

It was a proud day for Janet and Christina; though Janet, guided by some fine instinct,

remained in her own home, and made no afternoon calls. "I don't want to force folk to say
either kind or unkind things to me," she said
to her daughter. "You know, Christina, it is
a deal harder to rejoice with them that rejoice
than to weep with them that weep. Sabrina
Roy, as soon as she got her eyes on Andrew in
his trimmings, perfectly changed colours with
envy; and we have been a speculation to far
and near, more than one body saying we were
going fairly to the mischief with out extrava-
gance. They thought poverty had us under
her black thumb, and they did not think of the
hand of God, which was our surety."

However, that afternoon Janet had a great
many callers, and not a few came up the cliff
out of real kindness; for, doubt as we will,
there is a constant inflowing of God into
human affairs. And Janet, in her heart, did
not doubt her neighbours readily; she took the
homage rendered in a very pleased and gracious
manner, and she made a cup of tea and a little
feast for her company, and the clash and clat-
ter in the Binnie cottage that afternoon was
exceedingly full of good wishes and compliments. Indeed, as Janet reviewed them afterwards, they provoked from her a broad smile,
and she said with a touch of good-natured
criticism : —

"If we could make compliments into silk gowns, Christina, you and I would be bonnily clad for the rest of our lives. Nobody said a nattering word but poor Bella McLean, and she has been soured and sore kept down in the world by a ne'er-do-weel of a husband."

"She should try and guide him better," said Christina. "If he was my man, I would put him through his facings."

"*Toots*, Christina. You are over young in the marriage state to offer opinions about men folk. As far as I can see, every woman can guide a bad husband but the poor soul that has the ill-luck to have one. Open the Book now, and let us thank God for the good day He has given us."

CHAPTER X

AFTER this, the pleasant months went by with nothing but Andrew's and Jamie's visits to mark them, and, every now and then, a sough of sorrow from the big house of Braelands. And now that her own girl was so happily settled, Janet began to have a longing anxiety about poor Sophy. She heard all kinds of evil reports concerning the relations between her and her husband, and twice during the winter there was a rumour, hardly hushed up, of a separation between them.

Isobel Murray, to whom at first Sophy turned in her sorrow, had not responded to any later confidences. "My man told me to neither listen nor speak against Archie Braelands," she said to Janet. "We have our own boat to guide, and Sophy cannot be a friend to us; while it is very sure Braelands can be an enemy beyond our 'don't care.' Six little lads and lassies made folk mind their own business. And I'm no very sure but what Sophy's troubles

are Sophy's own making. At any rate, she
is n't faultless; you be to have both flint and
stone to strike fire."

"I 'll not hear you say the like of that, Isobel.
Sophy may be misguided and unwise, but there
is not a wrong thought in her heart. The bit
vanity of the young thing was her only fault, and
I 'm thinking she has paid sorely for it."

All winter such vague and miserable bits of
gossip found their way into the fishing-village,
and one morning in the following spring, Janet
met a young girl who frequently went to Braelands House with fresh fish. She was then on
her way home from such an errand, and Janet
fancied there was a look of unusual emotion on
her broad, stolid face.

"Maggie-Ann," she said, stopping her, "where
have you been this morning?"

"Up to Braelands."

"And what did you see or hear tell of?"

"I saw nothing; but I heard more than I
liked to hear."

"About Mistress Braelands? You know,
Maggie-Ann, that she is my own flesh and blood,
and I be to feel her wrongs my wrongs."

"Surely, Janet. There had been a big stir,
and you could feel it in the very air of the
house. The servants were feared to speak or
to step, and when the door opened, the sound

of angry words and of somebody crying was plain to be heard. Jean Craigie, the cook, told me it was about the Dower House. The mistress wants to get away from her mother-in-law, and she had been begging her husband to go and live in the Dower House with her, since Madame would not leave them their own place."

"She is right," answered Janet boldly. "I would n't live with that fine old sinner myself, and I think there are few women in Fife I could n't talk back to if I wanted. Sophy ought never to have bided with her for a day. They have no business under the same roof. A baby and a popish inquisitor would be as well matched."

It had, indeed, come at last to Sophy's positive refusal to live longer with her mother-in-law. In a hundred ways the young wife felt her inability to cope with a woman so wise and so wicked, and she had finally begun to entreat Archie to take her away from Braelands. The man was in a strait which could end only in anger. He was completely under his mother's influence, while Sophy's influence had been gradually weakened by Madame's innuendos and complaints, her pity for Archie, and her tattle of visitors. These things were bad enough; but Sophy's worst failures came from within herself. She had been snubbed and laughed at, scolded

219

and corrected, until she had lost all spontaneity, and all the grace and charm of her natural manner. This condition would not have been so readily brought about, had she retained her health and her flower-like beauty. But after the birth of her child she faded slowly away. She had not the strength for a constant, never-resting assertion of her rights, and nothing less would have availed her; nor had she the metal brightness to expose or circumvent the false and foolish positions in which Madame habitually placed her.

Little by little, the facts of the unhappy case leaked out, and were warmly commented on by the fisher-families with whom Sophy was connected either by blood or friendship. Her father's shipmates were many of them living, and she had cousins of every degree among the nets — men and women who did not forget the motherless, fatherless lassie who had played with their own children. These people made Archie feel their antagonism. They would neither take his money, nor give him their votes, nor lift their bonnets to his greeting. And though such honest, primitive feelings were proper enough, they did not help Sophy. On the contrary, they strengthened Madame's continual assertion that her son's marriage had ruined his public career and political prospects.

Still there is nothing more wonderful than the tugs and twists the marriage-tie will bear. There were still days in which Archie — either from love, or pity, or contradiction, or perhaps from a sense of simple justice — took his wife's part so positively that Madame must have been discouraged if she had been a less understanding woman. As it was, she only smiled at such fitful affection, and laid her plans a little more carefully. And as the devil strengthens the hands of those who do his work, Madame received a potent reinforcement in the return home of her nearest neighbour, Miss Marion Glamis. As a girl, she had been Archie's friend and playmate; then she had been sent to Paris for her education, and afterwards travelled extensively with her father, who was a man of very comfortable fortune. Marion herself had a private income, and Madame had been accustomed to believe that when Archie married, he would choose Marion Glamis for his wife.

She was a tall, high-coloured, rather mannish-looking girl, handsome in form, witty in speech, and disposed towards field sports of every kind. She disliked Sophy on sight, and Madame perceived it, and easily worked on the girl's worst feelings. Besides, Marion had no lover at the time, and she had come home with the idea of

Archie Braelands filling such imagination as she possessed. To find herself supplanted by a girl of low birth, " without a single advantage," as she said frankly to Archie's mother, provoked and humiliated her. " She has not beauty, nor grace, nor wit, nor money, nor any earthly thing to recommend her to Archie's notice. Was the man under a spell? " she asked.

" Indeed she had a kind of beauty and grace when Archie married her," answered Madame; " I must admit that. But bringing her to Brae-lands was like transplanting a hedge flower into a hot-house. She has just wilted ever since."

" Has she been noticed by Archie's friends at all? "

" I have taken good care she did not see much of Archie's friends, and her ill health has been a splendid excuse for her seclusion. Yet it was strange how much the few people she met admired her. Lady Blair goes into italics every time she comes here about ' The Beauty,' and the Bells, and Curries, and Cupars, have done their best to get her to visit them. I knew better than permit such folly. She would have told all sorts of things, and raised the country side against me; though, really, no one will ever know what I have gone through in my efforts to ' lick the cub into shape! ' "

Marion laughed, and, Archie coming in at that

moment, she launched all her high spirits and catches and witticisms at him. Her brilliancy and colour and style were very effective, and there was a sentimental remembrance for the foundation of a flirtation which Marion very cleverly took advantage of, and which Archie was not inclined to deny. His life was monotonous, he was ennuyé, and this bold, bright incarnation, with her half disguised admiration for himself, was an irresistible new interest.

So their intimacy soon became frequent and friendly. There were horseback rides together in the mornings, sails in the afternoons, and duets on the piano in the evenings. Then her Parisian toilets made poor Sophy's Largo dresses look funnily dowdy, and her sharp questions and affected ignorances of Sophy's meanings and answers were cleverly aided by Madame's cold silences, lifted brows, and hopeless acceptance of such an outside barbarian. Long before a dinner was over, Sophy had been driven into silence, and it was perhaps impossible for her to avoid an air of offence and injury, so that Marion had the charming in her own hands. After dinner, Admiral Glamis and Madame usually played a game of chess, and Archie sang or played duets with Marion, while Sophy, sitting sadly unnoticed and unemployed, watched her husband give to his companion such smiles and careful attentions as he had used to win her own heart.

What regrets and fears and feelings of wrong troubled her heart during these unhappy summer evenings, God only knew. Sometimes her presence seemed to be intolerable to Madame, who would turn to her and say sharply: "You are worn out, Sophy, and it is hardly fair to impose your weariness and low spirits on us. Had you not better go to your room?" Occasionally, Sophy refused to notice this covert order, and she fancied that there was generally a passing expression of pleasure on her husband's face at her rebellion. More frequently, she was glad to escape the slow, long torture, and she would rise, and go through the formality of shaking hands with each person and bidding each "good-night" ere she left the room. "Fisher manners," Madame would whisper impatiently to Marion. "I cannot teach her a decent effacement of her personality." For this little ceremony always ended in Archie's escorting her upstairs, and so far he had never neglected this formal deference due his wife. Sometimes too he came back from the duty very distrait and unhappy-looking, a circumstance always noted by Madame with anger and scorn.

To such a situation, any tragedy was a possible

culmination, and day by day there was a more reckless abuse of its opportunities. Madame, when alone with Sophy, did not now scruple to regret openly the fact that Marion was not her daughter-in-law, and if Marion happened to be present, she gave way to her disappointment in such ejaculations as —

" Oh! Marion Glamis, why did you stay away so long? Why did you not come home before Archie's life was ruined?" And the girl would sigh and answer: " Is not my life ruined also? Could any one have imagined Archie Braelands would have an attack of insanity?" Then Sophy, feeling her impotence between the tongues of her two enemies, would rise and go away, more or less angrily or sadly, followed through the hall and half-way upstairs by the snickering, confidential laughter of their common ridicule.

At the latter end of June, Admiral Glamis proposed an expedition to Norway. They were to hire a yacht, select a merry party, and spend July and August sailing and fishing in the cool fiords of that picturesque land. Archie took charge of all the arrangements. He secured a yacht, and posted a notice in the Public House of Pittendurie for men to sail her. He had no doubt of any number of applications; for the work was light and pleasant, and much better paid than any fishing-job. But not a man presented himself, and not even when Archie sought out the best sailors and those accustomed to the cross seas between Scotland and Norway, could he induce any one to take charge of the yacht and man her. The Admiral's astonishment at Archie's lack of influence among his own neighbours and tenants was not very pleasant to bear, and Marion openly said : —

"They are making cause with your wife, Archie, against you. They imagine themselves very loyal and unselfish. Fools! a few extra sovereigns would be much better."

"But why make cause for my wife against me, Marion?" asked Archie.

"You know best; ask Madame, she is my authority," and she shrugged her shoulders and went laughing from his side.

Nothing in all his married life had so annoyed Archie as this dour displeasure of men who had always before been glad to serve him. Madame was indignant, sorrowful, anxious, everything else that could further irritate her angry son; and poor Sophy might well have prayed in those days "deliver me from my friends!" But at length the yacht was ready for sea, and Archie ran upstairs in the middle of one hot afternoon to bid his wife "goodbye!"

She was resting on her bed, and he never forgot the eager, wistful, longing look of the wasted white face on the white pillow. He told her to take care of herself for his sake. He told her not to let any one worry or annoy her. He kissed her tenderly, and then, after he had closed the door, he came back and kissed her again; and there were days coming in which it was some comfort to him to remember this trifling kindness.

"You will not forget me, Archie?" she asked sadly.

"I will not, sweetheart," he answered.

"You will write me a letter when you can, dear?"

"I will be sure to do so."

"You — you — you will love me best of all?"

"How can I help it? Don't cry now. Send me away with a smile."

"Yes, dear. I will try and be happy, and try and get well."

"I am sorry you cannot go with us, Sophy."

"I am sorry too, Archie; but I could not bear the knocking about, and the noise and bustle, and the merry-making. I should only spoil your pleasure. I wouldn't like to do that, dear. Good-bye, and good-bye."

For a few minutes he was very miserable. A sense of shame came over him. He felt that he was unkind, selfish, and quite unworthy of the tender love given him. But in half an hour he was out at sea, Marion was at his side, the Admiral was consulting him about the cooling of the dinner wines, the skipper was promising them a lively sail with a fair wind — and the white, loving face went out of his memory, and out of his consideration.

Yet while he was sipping wine and singing songs with Marion Glamis, and looking with admiration into her rosy, glowing face, Sophy was suffering all the slings and arrows of Madame's outrageous hatred. She complained all dinner-time, even while the servants were present, of the deprivation she had to endure for Sophy's sake. The fact was she had not been invited to join the yachting-party, two very desirable ladies having refused to spend two months in her society. But she ignored this fact, and insisted on the fiction that she had been compelled to remain at home to look after Sophy.

"I wish you had gone! Oh, I wish you had gone and left me in peace!" cried the poor wife at last in a passion. "I could have been happy if I had been left to myself."

"And your low relations! You have made mischief enough with them for Archie, poor fellow! Don't tell me that you make no complaints. The shameful behaviour of those vulgar fishermen, refusing to sail a yacht for Braelands, is proof positive of your underhand ways."

"My relations are not low. They would scorn to do the low, cruel, wicked things some people who call themselves 'high-born' do all the time. But low or high, they are mine, and while Archie is away, I intend to see them as often as I can."

This little bit of rebellion was the one thing in which she could show herself Mistress of Braelands; for she knew that she could rely on Thomas to bring the carriage to her order. So the next morning she went very early to call on Griselda Kilgour. Griselda had not seen her niece for some time, and she was shocked at the change in her appearance; indeed, she could hardly refrain the exclamations of pity and fear that flew to her lips.

"Send the carriage to the *Queen's Arms*," she said, "and stay with me all day, Sophy, my dear."

"Very well, Aunt, I am tired enough. Let me lie down on the sofa, and take off my bonnet and cloak. My clothes are just a weight and a weariness."

"Aren't you well, dearie?"

"I must be sick someway, I think. I can't sleep, and I can't eat; and I am that weak I have n't the strength or spirit to say a word back to Madame, however ill her words are to me."

"I heard that Braelands had gone away?"

"Aye, for two months."

"With the Glamis crowd?"

"Yes."

"Why did n't you go too?"

"I could n't thole the sail, nor the company."

"Do you like Miss Glamis?"

"I 'm feared I hate her. Oh! Aunt, she makes love to Archie before my very eyes; and Madame tells me morning, noon, and night, that she was his first love and ought to have married him."

"I would n't stand the like of that. But Archie is not changed to you, dearie?"

"I cannot say he is; but what man can be aye with a fond woman, bright and bonnie, and not think of her as he should n't think? I 'm not blaming Archie much. It is Madame and Miss Glamis, and above all my own shortcomings. I can't talk, I can't dress, I can't walk, nor in any way act, as that set of women do. I am like a fish out of its element. It is bonnie enough in the water; but it only flops and dies if you take it out of the water and put it on the dry land. I wish I had never seen Archie Braelands! If I had n't, I would have married Andrew Binnie, and been happy and well enough."

"You were hearing that he is now Captain Binnie of the Red-White Fleet?"

"Aye, I heard. Madame was reading about it in the Largo paper. Andrew is a good man, Aunt. I am glad of his good luck."

"Christina is well married too. You were hearing of that?"

"Aye; but tell me all about it."

So Griselda entered into a narration which lasted until Sophy slipped into a deep slumber. And whether it was simply the slumber of utter exhaustion, or whether it was the sweet oblivion which results from a sense of peace long denied, or perhaps the union of both these conditions, the result was that she lay wrapped in an almost lethargic sleep for many hours. Twice Thomas came with the carriage, and twice Griselda sent him away. And the man shook his head sadly and said:—

"Let her alone; I would n't be the one to wake her up for all my place is worth. It may be a health sleep."

"Aye, it may be," answered Griselda, "but I have heard old folk say that such black, deep sleep is sent to fit the soul for some calamity lying in wait for it. It won't be lucky to wake her anyway."

"No, and I am thinking nothing worse can come to the little mistress than the sorrow she is tholing now. I 'll be back in an hour, Miss Kilgour."

Thus it happened that it was late in the afternoon when Sophy returned to her home, and her rest had so refreshed her that she was more than usually able to hold her own with Madame. Many unpardonable words were said on both sides; and the quarrel, thus early inaugurated, raged from day to day, either in open recrimination, or in a still more distressing interference with all Sophy's personal desires and occupations. The servants were, in a measure, compelled to take part in the unnatural quarrel; and before three weeks were over, Sophy's condition was one of such abnormal excitement that she was hardly any longer accountable for her actions. The final blow was struck while she was so little able to bear it. A letter from Archie, posted in Christiania and addressed to his wife, came one morning. As Sophy was never able to come down to breakfast, Madame at once appropriated the letter. When she had read it and finished her breakfast, she went to Sophy's room.

"I have had a letter from Archie," she said.

"Was there none for me?"

"No; but I thought you might like to know

that Archie says he never was so happy in all
his life. The Admiral, and Marion, and he, are
in Christiania for a week or two, and enjoying
themselves every minute of the time. Dear
Marion! *She* knows how to make Archie happy.
It is a great shame I could not be with them."

"Is there any message for me?"

"Not a word. I suppose Archie knew I
should tell you all that it was necessary for
you to know."

"Please go away; I want to go to sleep."

"You want to cry. You do nothing but
sleep and cry, and cry and sleep; no wonder
you have tired Archie's patience out."

"I have not tired Archie out. Oh, I wish
he was here! I wish he was here!"

"He will be back in five or six weeks, unless
Marion persuades him to go to the Mediter-
ranean — and, as the Admiral is so fond of the
sea, that move is not unlikely."

"Please go away."

"I shall be only too happy to do so."

Now it happened that the footman, in taking
in the mail, had noticed the letter for Sophy,
and commented on it in the kitchen; and every
servant in the house had been glad for the joy
it would bring to the lonely, sick woman. So
there was nothing remarkable in her maid saying, as she dressed her mistress: —

"I hope Mr. Braelands is well; and though I say it as perhaps I should n't say it, we was all pleased at your getting Master's letter this morning. We all hope it will make you feel brighter and stronger, I 'm sure."

"The letter was Madame's letter, not mine, Leslie."

"Indeed, it was not, ma'am. Alexander said himself, and I heard him, ' there is a long letter for Mrs. Archibald this morning,' and we were all that pleased as never was."

"Are you sure, Leslie?"

"Yes, I am sure."

"Go down-stairs and ask Alexander."

Leslie went and came back immediately with Alexander's positive assertion that the letter was directed to *Mrs. Archibald Braelands.* Sophy made no answer, but there was a swift and remarkable change in her appearance and manner. She put her physical weakness out of her consideration, and with a flush on her cheeks and a flashing light in her eyes, she went down to the parlour. Madame had a caller with her, a lady of not very decided position, who was therefore eager to please her patron; but Sophy was beyond all regard for such conventionalities as she had been ordered to observe. She took no notice of the visitor, but going straight to Madame, she said : —

"You took my letter this morning. You had no right to take it; you had no right to read it; you had no right to make up lies from it and come to my bedside with them. Give me my letter."

Madame turned to her visitor. "You see this impossible creature!" she cried. "She demands from me a letter that never came."

"It did come. You have my letter. Give it to me."

"My dear Sophy, go to your room. You are not in a fit state to see any one."

"Give me my letter. At least, let me see the letter that came."

"I shall do nothing of the kind. If you choose to suspect me, you must do so. Can I make your husband write to you?"

"He did write to me."

"Mrs. Stirling, do you wonder now at my son's running away from his home?"

"Indeed I am fairly astonished at what I see and hear."

"Sophy, you foolish woman, do not make any greater exhibit of yourself that you have done. For heaven's sake, go to your own room. I have only my own letter, and I told you all of importance in it."

"Every servant in the house knows that the letter was mine."

"What the servants know is nothing to me. Now, Sophy, I will stand no more of this; either you leave the room, or Mrs. Stirling and I will do so. Remember that you have betrayed yourself. I am not to blame."

"What do you mean, Madame?"

"I mean that you may have hallucinations, but that you need not exhibit them to the world. For my son's sake, I demand that you go to your room."

"I want my letter. For God's sake, have pity on me, and give me my letter!"

Madame did not answer, but she took her friend by the arm and they left the room together. In the hall Madame saw a servant, and she said blandly:—

"Go and tell Leslie to look after her mistress; she is in the parlour. And you may also tell Leslie that if she allows her to come down again in her present mood, she will be dismissed."

"Poor thing!" said Mrs. Stirling. "You must have your hands full with her, Madame. Nobody had any idea of such a tragedy as this, though I must say I have heard many wonder about the lady's seclusion."

"You see the necessity for it. However, we do not wish any talk on the subject."

Slowly it came to Sophy's comprehension

that she had been treated like an insane woman, and her anger, though quiet, was of that kind that means action of some sort. She went to her room, but it was only to recall the wrong upon wrong, the insult upon insult she had received.

"I will go away from it all," she said. "I will go away until Archie returns. I will not sleep another night under the same roof with that wicked woman. I will stay away till I die, ere I will do it."

Usually she had little strength for much movement, but at this hour she felt no physical weakness. She made Leslie bring her a street costume of brown cloth, and she carefully put into her purse all the money she had. Then she ordered the carriage and rode as far as her aunt Kilgour's. "Come for me in an hour, Thomas," she said, and then she entered the shop.

"Aunt, I am come back to you. Will you let me stay with you till Archie gets home? I can bide yon dreadful old woman no longer."

"Meaning Madame Braelands?"

"She is just beyond all things. This morning she has kept a letter that Archie wrote me; and she has told me a lot of lies in its place. I 'm not able to thole her another hour."

"I 'll tell you what, Sophy, Madame was

here since I saw you, and she says you are neither to be guided nor endured. I don't know who to believe."

"Oh! aunt, aunt, you know well I would n't tell you a lie. I am so miserable! For God's sake, take me in!"

"I 'd like to, Sophy, but I 'm not free to do so."

"You 're putting Madame's bit of siller and the work she 's promised you from the Glamis girl before my heart-break. Oh, how can you?"

"Sophy, you have lived with me, and I saw you often dissatisfied and unreasonable for nothing at all."

"I was a bit foolish lassie then. I am a poor, miserable, sick woman now."

"You have no need to be poor, and miserable, and sick. I won't encourage you to run away from your home and your duty. At any rate, bide where you are till your husband comes back. I would be wicked to give you any other advice."

"You mean that you won't let me come and stay with you?"

"No, I won't. I would be your worst enemy if I did."

"Then good-bye. You will maybe be sorry some day for the ' No ' you have just said."

" She went slowly out of the store, and

Griselda was very unhappy, and called to her to come back and wait for her carriage. She did not heed or answer, but walked with evident purpose down a certain street. It led her to the railway station, and she went in and took a ticket for Edinburgh. She had hardly done so when the train came thundering into the station; she stepped into it, and in a few minutes was flying at express-rate to her destination. She had relatives in Edinburgh, and she thought she knew their dwelling-place, having called on them with her Aunt Kilgour when they were in that city, just previous to her marriage. But she found that they had removed, and no one in the vicinity knew to what quarter of the town. She was too tired to pursue inquiries, or even to think any more that day, and she went to a hotel and tried to rest and sleep. In the morning she remembered that her mother's cousin, Jane Anderson, lived in Glasgow at some number in Monteith Row. The Row was not a long one, even if she had to go from house to house to find her relative. So she determined to go on to Glasgow.

She felt ill, strangely ill; she was in a burning fever and did not know it. Yet she managed to get into the proper train, and to retain her consciousness for sometime afterwards, ere she succumbed to the inevitable consequences of her condition. Before the train reached its destination, however, she was in a desperate state, and the first action of the guard was to call a carriage and send her to a hospital.

After this kindness had been done, Sophy was dead to herself and the world for nearly three weeks. She remembered nothing, she knew nothing, she spoke only in the most disconnected and puzzling manner. For her speech wandered between the homely fisher-life of her childhood and the splendid social life of Braelands. Her personality was equally perplexing. The clothing she wore was of the finest quality; her rings, and brooch, and jewelled watch, indicated wealth and station; yet her speech, especially during the fever, was that of the people, and as she began to help herself, she had little natural actions that showed the want of early polite breeding. No letter or card, no name or address of any kind, was found on her person; she appeared to be as absolutely lost as a stone dropped into the deep sea.

And when she came to herself and realised where she was, and found out from her attendant the circumstances under which she had been brought to the hospital, she was still more reticent. For her first thought related to the annoyance Archie would feel at her detention in a public hospital; her second, to the unmerciful use Madame would make of the circumstance. She could not reason very clearly, but her idea was to find her cousin and gain her protection, and then, from that more respectable covert, to write to her husband. She might admit her illness — indeed, she would be almost compelled to do that, for she had fallen away so much, and had had her hair cut short during the height of the fever — but Archie and Madame must not know that she had been in a public hospital. For fisher-people have a singular dislike to public charity of any kind; they help one another. And, to Sophy's intelligence, the hospital episode was a disgrace that not even her insensibility could quite excuse.

Several weeks passed in that long, spotless, white room full of suffering, before Sophy was able to stand upon her feet, before indeed she began to realise the passage of time, and the consequences which must have followed her long absence and silence. But all her efforts at writing were failures. The thought she wished to express slipped off into darkness as soon as she tried to write it; her vision failed her, her hands failed her; she could only sink back upon her pillow and lie inert and almost indifferent for hours afterwards. And as the one letter she wished to write was to Archie, she could not depute it to any one else. Besides, the nurse would tell *where* she was, and that was a circumstance she must at all hazards keep to herself. It had been hot July weather when she was first placed on her hard, weary bed of suffering, it was the end of September when she was able to leave the hospital. Her purse with its few sovereigns in it was returned to her, and the doctor told her kindly, if she had any friends in the world, to go at once to their care.

"You have talked a great deal of the sea and the boats," he said; "get close to the sea if you can; it is perhaps the best and the only thing for you."

She thanked him and answered: "I am going to the Fife coast. I have friends there, I think." She put out a little wasted hand, and he clasped it with a sigh.

"So young, so pretty, so good," he said to the nurse, as they stood watching her walk very feebly and unsteadily away.

"I will give her three months at the longest, if she has love and care. I will give her three weeks — nay, I will say three days, if she has to care for herself, or if any particular trouble come to her."

Then they turned from the window, and Sophy hired a cab and went to Monteith Row to try and find her friends. She wanted to write to her husband and ask him to come for her. She thought she could do this best from her cousin's home. "I will give her a bonnie ring or two, and I will tell her the whole truth; and she will be sure to stand by me, for there is nothing wrong to stand by, and blood is aye thicker than water." And then her thoughts wandered on to a contingency that brought a flush of pain to her cheeks. "Besides, maybe Archie might have an ill-thought put into his head, and then the doctors and nurses in the hospital could tell him what would make all clear." She went through many of the houses, inquiring for Ellen Montgomery, but could not find her, and she was finally obliged to go to a hotel and rest. "I will take the lave of the houses in the morning," she thought, "it is aye the last thing that is the right thing; everybody finds that out."

That evening, however, something happened which changed all her ideas and intentions. She went into the hotel parlour and sat down; there were some newspapers on the table, and she lifted one. It was an Edinburgh paper, but the first words her eyes fell on was her husband's name. Her heart leaped up at the sight of it, and she read the paragraph. Then the paper dropped from her hands. She felt that she was going to faint, and by a supreme effort of will she recalled her senses and compelled them to stay and suffer with her. Again, and then again, she read the paragraph, unable at first to believe what she did read; for it was a notice, signed by her husband, advising the world in general that she had voluntarily left his home, and that he would no longer be responsible for any debt she might contract in his name. To her childlike, ignorant nature, this public exposure of her was a final act. She felt that it was all the same as a decree of divorce. "Archie had cast her off; Madame had at last parted them." For an hour she sat still in a very stupour of despair.

"But something might yet be done; yes, something must be done. She would go instantly to Fife; she would tell Archie everything. He could not blame her for being sick and beyond reason or knowledge. The doctors and nurses of the hospital would certify to the truth of all she said." Ah! she had only to look in a mirror to know that her own wasted face and form would have been testimony enough.

That night she could not move, she had done

all that it was possible for her to do that day; but on the morrow she would be rested and she might trust herself to the noise and bustle of the street and railway. The day was well on before she found strength to do this; but at length she found herself on the direct road to Largo, though she could hardly tell how it had been managed. As she approached the long chain of Fife fishing-villages, she bought the newspaper most widely read in them; and, to her terror and shame, found the same warning to honest folk against her. She was heart-sick. "With this barrier between Archie and herself, how could she go to Braelands? How could she face Madame? What mockery would be made of her explanations? No, she must see Archie alone. She must tell him the whole truth, somewhere beyond Madame's contradiction and influence. Whom should she go to? Her aunt Kilgour had turned her away, even before this disgrace. Her cousin Isobel's husband had asked her not to come to his house and make loss and trouble for him. If she went direct to Braelands, and Archie happened to be out of the house, Madame would say such things of her before every one as could never be unsaid. If she went to a hotel, she would be known, and looked at, and whispered about, and maybe slighted. What must she do?

Where could she see her husband best?" She
was at her wit's end. She was almost at the
end of her physical strength and consciousness.
And in this condition, two men behind her
began to talk to the rustle of their turning
newspapers.

"This is a queer-like thing about Braelands
and his wife," said one.

"It is a very bad thing. If the wife has
gane awa', she has been driven awa' by bad
usage. There is an old woman at Braelands
that is as evil-hearted as if she had slipped out
o' hell for a few years. Traill's girl was good
and bonnie; she was too good, or she would
have held her ain side better."

"That may be; but there is a reason deeper
than that. The man is wanting to marry the
Glamis girl. He has already began a suit for
divorce, I hear. Man, man, there is always a
woman at the bottom of every sin and trouble!"

Then they began to speak of the crops and
the shooting, and Sophy listened in vain for
more intelligence. But she had heard enough.
Her soul cried out against the hurry and shame
of the steps taken in the matter. "So cruel
as Archie is!" she sighed. "He might have
looked for me! He might have found me even
in that awful hospital! He ought to have done
so, and taken me away and nursed me himself!

If he had loved me! If he had loved me, he would have done these things!" Despair chilled her very blood. She had a thought of going to Braelands, even if she died on its threshold; and then suddenly she remembered Janet Binnie.

As Janet's name came to her mind, the train stopped at Largo, and she slipped out among the hurrying crowd and took the shortest road to Pittenduric. It was then nearly dark, and the evening quite chill and damp; but there was now a decisive end before the dying woman. "She must reach Janet Binnie, and then leave all to her. She would bring Archie to her side. She would be sufficient for Madame. If this only could be managed while she had strength to speak, to explain, to put herself right in Archie's eyes, then she would be willing and glad to die." Step by step, she stumbled forward, full of unutterable anguish of heart, and tortured at every movement by an inability to get breath enough to carry her forward.

At last, at last, she came in sight of Janet's cottage. The cliff terrified her; but she must get up it, somehow. And as she painfully made step after step, a light shone through the open door and seemed to give her strength and welcome. Janet had been spending the evening with her daughter, and had sat with her until near her bedtime. She was doing her last household duties, and the last of all was to close the house-door. When she went to do this, a little figure crouched on the door-step, two weak hands clasped her round the knees, and the very shadow of a thin, pitiful voice sobbed : —

"Janet! Take me in, Janet! Take me in to die! I'll not trouble you long — it is most over, Janet!"

CHAPTER XI

TOWARD this culmination of her troubles Archie had indeed contributed far too much, but yet not as much as Sophy thought. He had taken her part, he had sought for her, he had very reluctantly come to accept his mother's opinions. His trip had not been altogether the heaven Madame represented it. The Admiral had proved himself dictatorial and sometimes very disagreeable at sea; the other members of the party had each some unpleasant peculiarities which the cramped quarters and the monotony of yacht life developed. Some had deserted altogether, others grumbled more than was agreeable, and Marion's constant high spirits proved to be at times a great exaction.

Before the close of the pleasure voyage, Archie frequently went alone to remember the sweet, gentle affection of his wife, her delight in his smallest attentions, her instant recognition of his desires, her patient endeavours to please him, her resignation to all his neglect. Her image grew into his best imagination, and when he left the yacht at her moorings in Pittendurie Bay, he hastened to Sophy with the impatience of a lover who is also a husband.

Madame had heard of his arrival and was watching for her son. She met him at the door and he embraced her affectionately, but his first words were, "Sophy, I hope she is not ill. Where is she?"

"My dear Archie, no one knows. She left your home three weeks after you had sailed."

"My God, Mother, what do you mean?"

"No one knows why she left, no one knows or can find out where she went to. Of course, I have my suspicions."

"Sophy! Sophy! Sophy!" he cried, sinking into a chair and covering his face; but, whatever Madame's suspicions, she could not but see that Archie had not a doubt of his wife's honour. After a few minutes' silence, he turned to his mother and said:—

"You have scolded for once, Mother, more than enough. I am sure it is your unkindness that has driven my wife from her home. You promised me not to interfere with her little plans and pleasures."

"If I am to bear the blame of the woman's low tastes, I decline to discuss the matter;" and she left the room with an air of great offence.

Of course, if Madame would not discuss the matter with him, nothing remained but the making of such inquiries as the rest of the household could answer. Thomas readily told all he knew, which was the simple statement that "he took his mistress to her aunt's and left her there, and that when he returned for her, Miss Kilgour was much distressed and said she had already left." Archie then immediately sought Miss Kilgour, and from her learned the particulars of his wife's wretchedness, especially those points relating to the appropriated letter. He flushed crimson at this outrage, but made no remark concerning it.

"My one desire now," he said, "is to find out where Sophy has taken refuge. Can you give me any idea?"

"If she is not in Pittendurie, — and I can find no trace of her there, — then I think she may be in Edinburgh or Glasgow. You will mind she had cousins in Edinburgh, and she was very kind with them at the time of her marriage. I thought of them first of all, and I wrote three letters to them; but there has been no answer to any of the three. She has friends in Glasgow, but I am sure she had no knowledge as to where they lived. Besides, I got their address from kin in Aberdeen and wrote there also, and they answered me and said they

had never seen or heard tell of Sophy. Here
is their letter."

Archie read it carefully and was satisfied
that Sophy was not in Glasgow. The silence
of the Edinburgh cousins was more promising,
and he resolved to go at once to that city and
interview them. He did not even return to
Braelands, but took the next train southward.
Of course his inquiries utterly failed. He
found Sophy's relatives, but their air of amazement and their ready and positive denial of all
knowledge of his lost wife were not to be
doubted. Then he returned to Largo. He
assured himself that Sophy was certainly in
hiding among the fisher-folk in Pittendurie,
and that he would only have to let it be known
that he had returned for her to appear. Indeed
she must have seen the yacht at anchor, and
he fully expected to find her on the door-step
waiting for him. As he approached Braelands,
he fancied her arms round his neck, and saw
her small, wistful, flushing face against his
breast; but it was all a dream. The door was
closed, and when it admitted him there was
nothing but silence and vacant rooms. He was
nearly distracted with sorrow and anger, and
Madame had a worse hour than she ever remembered when Archie asked her about the fatal
letter that had been the active cause of trouble.

"The letter was Sophy's," he said passionately, "and you knew it was. How then could you be so shamefully dishonourable as to keep it from her?"

"If you choose to reproach me on mere servants' gossip, I cannot prevent you."

"It is not servants' gossip. I know by the date on which Sophy left home that it must have been the letter I wrote her from Christiania. It was a disgraceful, cruel thing for you to do. I can never look you in your face again, Mother. I do not feel that I can speak to you, or even see you, until my wife has forgiven both you and myself. Oh, if I only knew where to look for her!"

"She is not far to seek; she is undoubtedly among her kinsfolk at Pittendurie. You may remember, perhaps, how they felt toward you before you went away. After you went, she was with them continually."

"Then Thomas lies. He says he never took her anywhere but to her aunt Kilgour's."

"I think Thomas is more likely to lie than I am. If you have strength to bear the truth, I will tell you what I am convinced of."

"I have strength for anything but this wretched suspense and fear."

"Very well, then, go to the woman called Janet Binnie; you may recollect, if you will,

. that her son Andrew was Sophy's ardent **lover** — so much so, that her marriage to you nearly killed him. He has become a **captain** lately, wears gold buttons and bands, and is really a very handsome and important man in the opinion of such people as your wife. I believe Sophy is either in his mother's house or else she has gone to — London."

"Why London?"

"Captain Binnie sails continually to London. Really, Archie, there are none so blind as those who won't see."

"I will not believe such a thing of Sophy. She is as pure and innocent as a little child."

Madame laughed scornfully. "She is as pure and innocent as those baby-faced women usually are. As a general rule, the worst creature in the world is a saint in comparison. What did Sophy steal out at night for? Tell me that. Why did she walk to Pittendurie so often? Why did she tell me she was going to walk to her aunt's, and then never go?"

"Mother, Mother, are you telling me the truth?"

"Your inquiry is an insult, Archie. And your blindness to Sophy's real feelings is one of the most remarkable things I ever saw. Can you not look back and see that ever since she married you she has regretted and fretted about the step? Her heart is really with her fisher and sailor lover. She only married you for what you could give her; and having got what you could give her, she soon ceased to prize it, and her love went back to Captain Binnie,— that is, if it had ever left him."

Conversation based on these shameful fabrications was continued for hours, and Madame, who had thoroughly prepared herself for it, brought one bit of circumstantial evidence after another to prove her suspicions. The wretched husband was worked to a fury of jealous anger not to be controlled. "I will search every cottage in Pittendurie," he said in a rage. "I will find Sophy, and then kill her and myself."

"Don't be a fool, Archibald Braclands. Find the woman, — that is necessary, — then get a divorce from her, and marry among your own kind. Why should you lose your life, or even ruin it, for a fisherman's old love? In a year or two you will have forgotten her and thrown the whole affair behind your back."

It is easy to understand how a conversation pursued for hours in this vein would affect Archie. He was weak and impulsive, ready to suspect whatever was suggested, jealous of his own rights and honour, and on the whole of that pliant nature which a strong, positive woman like Madame could manipulate like wax. He walked his room all night in a frenzy of jealous love. Sophy lost to him had acquired a sudden charm and value beyond all else in life; he longed for the morning; for Madame's positive opinions had thoroughly convinced him, and he felt a great deal more sure than she did that Sophy was in Pittendurie. And yet, after every such assurance to himself, his inmost heart asked coldly, "Why then has she not come back to you?"

He could eat no breakfast, and as soon as he thought the village was awake, he rode rapidly down to Pittendurie. Janet was alone; Andrew was somewhere between Fife and London; Christina was preparing her morning meal in her own cottage. Janet had already eaten hers, and she was washing her tea-cup and plate and singing as she did so, —

> " I cast my line in Largo Bay,
>   And fishes I caught nine;
> There's three to boil, and three to fry,
>   And three to bait the line,"

when she heard a sharp rap at her door. The rap was not made with the hand; it was per-emptory and unusual, and startled Janet. She put down the plate she was wiping, ceased singing, and went to the door. The Master of Braelands was standing there. He had his

short riding-whip in his hand, and Janet understood at once that he had struck her house door
with the handle of it. She was offended at
this, and she asked dourly: —

"Well, sir, your bidding?"

"I came to see my wife. Where is she?"

"You ought to know that better than any
other body. It is none of my business."

"I tell you she has left her home."

"I have no doubt she had the best of good
reasons for doing so."

"She had no reason at all."

Janet shrugged her shoulders, smiled with
scornful disbelief, and looked over the tossing
black waters.

"Woman, I wish to go through your house,
I believe my wife is in it."

"Go through my house? No indeed. Do
you think I'll let a man with a whip in his
hand go through my house after a poor frightened bird like Sophy? No, no, not while my
name is Janet Binnie."

"I rode here; my whip is for my horse. Do
you think I would use it on any woman?"

"God knows, I don't."

"I am not a brute."

"You say so yourself."

"Woman, I did not come here to bandy
words with you."

"Man, I 'm no caring to hear another word you have to say; take yourself off my doorstone," and Janet would have shut the door in his face, but he would not permit her.

"Tell Sophy to come and speak to me."

"Sophy is not here."

"She has no reason to be afraid of me."

"I should think not."

"Go and tell her to come to me then."

"She is not in my house. I wish she was."

"She *is* in your house."

"Do you dare to call me a liar? Man alive! Do it again, and every fisher-wife in Pittendurie will help me to give you your fairings."

"*Tush!* Let me see my wife."

"Take yourself off my doorstep, or it will be the worse for you."

"Let me see my wife."

"Coming here and chapping on my door — on Janet Binnie's door! — with a horsewhip!"

"There is no use trying to deceive me with bad words. Let me pass."

"Off with you! you poor creature, you! Sophy Traill had a bad bargain with the like of you, you drunken, lying, savage-like, wife-beating pretence o' a husband!"

"Mother! Mother!" cried Christina, coming hastily forward; "Mother, what are you saying at all?"

"The God's truth, Christina, that and nothing else. Ask the mean, perfectly unutterable scoundrel how he got beyond his mother's apron-strings so far as this?"

Christina turned to Braelands. "Sir," she said, "what's your will?"

"My wife has left her home, and I have been told she is in Mistress Binnie's house."

"She is not. We know nothing about the poor, miserable lass, God help her!"

"I cannot believe you."

"Please yourself anent believing me; but you had better be going, sir. I see Limmer Scott and Mistress Roy and a few more fish-wives looking this way."

"Let them look."

"Well, they have their own fashion of dealing with men who ill-use a fisher-lass. Sophy was born among them."

"You are a bad lot! altogether a bad lot!"

"Go now, and go quick, or we'll prove to you that we are a bad lot!" cried Janet. "I wouldn't myself think anything of putting you in a blanket and tossing you o'er the cliff into the water." And Janet, with arms akimbo and eyes blazing with anger, was not a comfortable sight.

So, with a smile of derision, Braelands turned his back on the women, walking with an affected deliberation which by no means hid the white feather from the laughing, jeering fisher-wives who came to their door at Janet's call for them, and whose angry mocking fol- lowed him until he was out of sight and hear- ing. Then there was a conclave in Janet's house, and every one told a different version of the Braelands trouble. In each case, how- ever, Madame was credited with the whole of the sorrow-making, though Janet stoutly asserted that "a man who was feared for his mother was n't fit to be a husband."

"Madame's tongue and temper is kindled from a coal out of hell," she said, "and that is the God's truth; but she could n't do ill with them, if Archie Braelands was n't a coward — a sneaking, trembling coward, that has n't the heart in him to stand between poor little Sophy and the most spiteful, hateful old sin- ner this side of the brimstone pit."

But though the birr and first flame of the village anger gradually cooled down, Janet's and Christina's hearts were hot and heavy within them, and they could not work, nor eat, nor sleep with any relish, for thinking of the poor little runaway wife. Indeed, in every cottage there was one topic of wonder and pity, and one sad lament when two or three of the women came together: "Poor Sophy! Poor

Sophy Braelands!" It was noticeable, however, that not a single woman had a wrong
thought of Sophy. Madame could easily suspect the worst; but the "worst" was an incredible thing to a fisher-wife. Some indeed
blamed her for not tholing her grief until her
husband came back; but not a single heart suspected her of a liaison with her old lover.

Archie, however, returned from his in-
effectual effort to find her with every suspicion strengthened. Madame could hardly have
hoped for a visit so completely in her favour;
and after it Archie was entirely under her
influence. It is true he was wretchedly de-
spondent; but he was also furiously angry.
He fancied himself the butt of his friends,
he believed every one to be talking about his
affairs, and, day by day, his sense of outrage
and dishonour pressed him harder and harder.
In a month he was quite ready to take legal
steps to release himself from such a doubtful
tie, and Madame, with his tacit permission,
took the first step towards such a consumma-
tion by writing with her own hand the notice
which had driven Sophy to despair.

While events were working towards this end,
Sophy was helpless and senseless in the Glasgow hospital. Archie's anger was grounded
on the fact that she must know of his return;

and yet she had neither come back to her home
nor sent him a line of communication. He
told himself that if she had written him one
line, he would have gone to the end of the
earth after her. And anon he told himself
that if she had been true to him, she would
have written or else come back to her home.
Say she was sick, she could have got some one
to use the pen or the telegraph for her. And
this round of reasoning, always led into the
same channel by Madame, finally assumed not
the changeable quality of argument, but the
positiveness of fact.

So the notice of her abandonment was sent
by the press far and wide, and yet there came
no protest against it; for Sophy had brought
to the hospital nothing by which she could
be identified, and as no hint of her personal
appearance was given, it was impossible to
connect her with it. Thus while its cruel
words linked suspicion with her name in every
household where they went, she lay ignorantly
passive, knowing nothing at all of the wrong
done her and of the unfortunate train of circumstances which finally forced her husband
to doubt her love and her honour. It was an
additional calamity that this angry message
of severance was the first thing that met her
consciousness when she was at all able to act.

Her childish ignorance and her primitive ideas aided only too well the impression of finality it gave. She put it beside all she had seen and heard of her husband's love for Marion Glamis, and the miserable certainty was plain to her. She knew she was dying, and a quiet place to die in and a little love to help her over the hard hour seemed to be all she could expect now; the thought of Janet and Christina was her last hope. Thus it was that Janet found her trembling and weeping on her doorstep; thus it was she heard that pitiful plaint, "Take me in, Janet! Take me in to die!"

Never for one moment did Janet think of refusing this sad petition. She sat down beside her; she laid Sophy's head against her broad loving breast; she looked with wondering pity at the small, shrunken face, so wan and ghost-like in the gray light. Then she called Christina, and Christina lifted Sophy easily in her arms, and carried her into her own house. "For we'll give Braelands no occasion against either her or Andrew," she said. Then they undressed the weary woman and made her a drink of strong tea; and after a little she began to talk in a quick, excited manner about her past life.

"I ran away from Braelands at the end of July," she said. "I could not bear the life

there another hour; I was treated before folk
as if I had lost my senses; I was treated when
I was alone as if I had no right in the house,
and as if my being in it was a mortal wrong
and misery to every one. And at the long last
the woman there kept Archie's letter from me,
and I was wild at that, and sick and trembling
all over; and I went to Aunt Griselda, and she
took Madame's part and would not let me
stay with her till Archie came back to protect me. What was I to do? I thought of my
cousins in Edinburgh and went there, and could
not find them. Then there was only Ellen
Montgomery in Glasgow, and I was ill and so
tired; but I thought I could manage to reach
her."

"And did n't you reach her, dearie?"

"No. I got worse and worse; and when I
reached Glasgow I knew nothing at all, and
they sent me to the hospital."

"Oh, Sophy! Sophy!"

"Aye, they did. What else could be, Janet?
No one knew who I was; I could not tell any
one. They were n't bad to me. I suffered,
but they did what they could to help me.
Such dreadful nights, Janet! Such long, awful
days! Week after week in which I knew
nothing but pain; I could not move myself;
I could not write to any one, for my thoughts

would not stay with me; and my sight went away, and I had hardly strength to live."

"Try and forget it, Sophy, darling," said Christina. "We will care for you now, and the sea-winds will blow health to you."

She shook her head sadly. "Only the winds of heaven will ever blow health to me, Christina," she answered; "I have had my death blow. I am going fast to them who have gone before me. I have seen my mother often, the last wee while. I knew it was my mother, though I do not remember her; she is waiting for her bit lassie. I shall not have to go alone; and His rod and staff will comfort me, I will fear no evil."

They kissed and petted and tried to cheer her, and Janet begged her to sleep; but she was greatly excited and seemed bent on excusing and explaining what she had done. "For I want you to tell Archie everything, Janet," she said. "I shall maybe never see him again; but you must take care that he has not a wrong thought of me."

"He'll get the truth and the whole truth from me, dearie."

"Don't scold him, Janet. I love him very much. It is not his fault."

"I don't know that."

"No, it is not. I wasn't home to Braelands

265

two days before Madame began to make fun of my talk, and my manners, and my dress, and of all I did and said. And she got Archie to tell me I must mind her, and try to learn how to be a fine lady like her; and I could not — I could not. And then she set Archie against me, and I was scolded just for nothing at all. And then I got ill, and she said I was only sulky and awkward; but I just could not learn the books I be to learn, nor walk as she showed me how to walk, nor talk like her, nor do anything at all she tried to make me do. Oh, the weary, weary days that I have fret myself through! Oh, the long, painful nights! I am thankful they can never, never come back."

"Then don't think of them now, Sophy. Try and rest yourself a bit, and to-morrow you shall tell me everything."

"To-morrow will be too late, can't you see that, Janet? I must clear myself to-night — now — or you won't know what to say to Archie."

"Was Archie kind to you, Sophy?"

"Sometimes he was that kind I thought I must be in the wrong, and then I tried again harder than ever to understand the weary books and do what Madame told me. Sometimes they made him cross at me, and I thought I must die with the shame and heartache from it. But it was not till Marion Glamis came back

266

that I lost all hope. She was Archie's first love, you know."

"She was nothing of the kind. I don't believe he ever cared a pin for her. You had the man's first love; you have it yet, if it is worth aught. He was here seeking you, dearie, and he was distracted with the loss of you."

"In the morning you will send for him, Janet, very early; and though I'll be past talking then, you will talk for me. You will tell him how Madame tortured me about the Glamis girl, how she kept my letters, and made Mrs. Stirling think I was not in my right mind," and so between paroxysms of pain and coughing, she went over and over the sad story of petty wrongs that had broken her heart, and driven her at last to rebellion and flight.

"Oh! my poor lassie, why didn't you come to Christina and me?"

"There was aye the thought of Andrew. Archie would have been angry, maybe, and I could only feel that I must get away from Braelands. When aunt failed me, something seemed to drive me to Edinburgh, and then on to Glasgow; but it was all right, you see, I have saved you and Christina for the last hour," and she clasped Christina's hand and laid her head closer to Janet's breast.

"And I would like to see the man or woman

that will dare to trouble you now, my bonnie bairn," said Janet. There was a sob in her voice, and she crooned kind words to the dying girl, who fell asleep at last in her arms. Then Janet went to the door, and stood almost gasping in the strong salt breeze; for the shock of Sophy's pitiful return had hurt her sorely. There was a full moon in the sky, and the cold, gray waters tossed restlessly under it. "Lord help us, we must bear what's sent!" she whispered; then she noticed a steamboat with closely reefed sails lying in the offing, and added thankfully, "There is 'The Falcon,' God bless her! And it's good to think that Andrew Binnie isn't far away; maybe he'll be wanted. I wonder if I ought to send a word to him; if Sophy wants to see him, she shall have her way; dying folk don't make any mistakes."

Now when Andrew came to anchor at Pittendurie, it was his custom to swing out a signal light, and if the loving token was seen, Janet and Christina answered by placing a candle in their windows. This night Janet put three candles in her window. "Andrew will wonder at them," she thought, "and maybe come on shore to find out whatever their meaning may be." Then she hurriedly closed the door. The night was cold, but it was more than that, — the air had the peculiar coldness that gives

sense of the supernatural; such coldness as
precedes the advent of a spirit. She was awed;
she opened her mouth as if to speak, but was
dumb; she put out her hands — but who can
arrest the invisible?

Sleep was now impossible. The very air of
the room was sensitive. Christina sat wide
awake on one side of the bed, Janet on the
other; they looked at each other frequently,
but did not talk. There was no sound but the
rising moans of the northeast wind, no light
but the glow of the fire and the shining of the
full moon looking out from the firmament as
from eternity. Sophy slept restlessly like one
in half-conscious pain, and when she awoke
before dawning, she was in a high fever and
delirious; but there was one incessant, gasping
cry for "Andrew!"

"Andrew! Andrew! Andrew!" she called
with fast failing breath, "Andrew, come and
go for Archie. Only you can bring him to
me." And Janet never doubted at this hour
what love and mercy asked for. "Folks may
talk if they want to," she said to Christina, "I
am going down to the village to get some one
to take a message to Andrew. Sophy shall
have her will at this hour if I can compass it."

The men of the village were mostly yet at
the fishing, but she found two old men who

willingly put out to "The Falcon" with the
message for her captain. Then she sent a
laddie for the nearest doctor, and she called
herself for the minister, and asked him to come
and see the sick woman; "forbye, minister,"
she added, "I'm thinking you will be the only
person in Pittendurie that will have the need-
ful control o' temper to go to Braelands with
the news." She did not specially hurry any
one, for, sick as Sophy was, she believed it
likely Archie Braelands and a good doctor
might give her such hope and relief as would
prolong her life a little while. "She is so
young," she thought, "and love and sea-breezes
are often a match for death himself."

The old men who had gone for Andrew were
much too infirm to get close to "The Falcon."
For with the daylight her work had begun, and
she was surrounded on all sides by a mêlée of
fishing-boats. Some were discharging their
boxes of fish; others were struggling to get
some point of vantage; others again fighting to
escape the uproar. The air was filled with the
roar of the waves and with the voices of men,
blending in shouts, orders, expostulations,
words of anger, and words of jest.

Above all this hubbub, Andrew's figure on
the steamer's bridge towered large and com-
manding, as he watched the trunks of fish

hauled on board, and then dragged, pushed, thrown, or kicked, as near the mouth of the hold as the blockade of trunks already shipped would permit. But, sharp as a crack of thunder, a stentorian voice called out: —

"Captain Binnie wanted! Girl dying in Pittendurie wants him!"

Andrew heard. The meaning of the three lights was now explained. He had an immediate premonition that it was Sophy, and he instantly deputed his charge to Jamie, and was at the gunwale before the shouter had repeated his alarm. To a less prompt and practised man, a way of reaching the shore would have been a dangerous and tedious consideration; but Andrew simply selected a point where a great wave would lift a small boat near to the level of the ship's bulwarks, and when this occurred, he leaped into her, and was soon going shoreward as fast as his powerful stroke at the oars could carry him.

When he reached Christina's cottage, Sophy had passed beyond all earthly care and love. She heeded not the tenderest words of comfort; her life was inexorably coming to its end; and every one of her muttered words was mysterious, important, wondrous, though they could make out nothing she said, save only that she talked about "angels resting in the hawthorn bowers." Hastily Christina gave Andrew the points of her sorrowful story, and then she suddenly remembered that a strange man had brought there that morning some large, important-looking papers which he had insisted on giving to the dying woman. Andrew, on examination, found them to be proceedings in the divorce case between Archibald Braclands and his wife Sophy Traill.

"Some one has recognised her in the train last night and then followed her here," he said pitifully. They were in a gey hurry with their cruel work. I hope she knows nothing about it."

"No, no, they did n't come till she was clean beyond the worriments of this life. She did not see the fellow who put them in her hands; she heard nothing he said to her."

"Then if she comes to herself at all, say nothing about them. What for should we tell her? Death will break her marriage very soon without either judge or jury."

"The doctor says in a few hours at the most."

"Then there is no time to lose. Say a kind ' farewell ' for me, Christina, if you find a minute in which she can understand it. I 'm off to Braclands," and he put the divorce papers in his pocket, and went down the cliff at a run.

When he reached the house, Archie was at the door on his horse and evidently in a hurry; but Andrew's look struck him on the heart like a blow. He dismounted without a word, and motioned to Andrew to follow him. They turned into a small room, and Archie closed the door. For a moment there was a terrible silence, then Andrew, with passionate sorrow, threw the divorce papers down on the table.

"You 'll not require, Braelands, to fash folk with the like of them; your wife is dying. She is at my sister's house. Go to her at once."

"What is that to you? Mind your own business, Captain Binnie."

"It is the business of every decent man to call comfort to the dying. Go and say the words you ought to say. Go before it is too late."

"Why is my wife at your sister's house?"

"God pity the poor soul, she had no other place to die in! For Christ's sake, go and say a loving word to her."

"Where has she been all this time? Tell me that, sir."

"Dying slowly in the public hospital at Glasgow."

"*My God!*"

"There is no time for words now; not a moment to spare. Go to your wife at once."

"She left me of her own free will. Why should I go to her now?"

"She did not leave you; she was driven away by devilish cruelty. And oh, man, man, go for your own sake then! To-morrow it will be too late to say the words you will weep to say. Go for your own sake. Go to spare yourself the black remorse that is sure to come if you don't go. If you don't care for your poor wife, go for your own sake!"

"I do care for my wife. I wished —"

"Haste you then, don't lose a moment! Haste you! haste you! If it is but one kind word before you part forever, give it to her. She has loved you well; she loves you yet; she is calling for you at the grave's mouth. Haste you, man! haste you!"

His passionate hurry drove like a wind, and Braelands was as straw before it. His horse stood there ready saddled; Andrew urged him to it, and saw him flying down the road to Pittendurie before he was conscious of his own efforts. Then he drew a long sigh, lifted the divorce papers and threw them into the blazing fire. A moment or two he watched them pass into smoke, and then he left the house with all the hurry of a soul anxious unto death. Half-way down the garden path, Madame Braelands stepped in front of him.

"What have you come here for?" she asked in her haughtiest manner.

"For Braelands."

"Where have you sent him to in such a black hurry?"

"To his wife. She is dying."

"Stuff and nonsense!"

"She is dying."

"No such luck for my house. The creature has been dying ever since he married her."

"*You* have been *killing her* ever since he married her. Give way, woman, I don't want to speak to you; I don't want to touch the very clothes of you. I think no better of you than God Almighty does, and He will ask Sophy's life at your hands."

"I shall tell Braelands of your impertinence. It will be the worse for you."

"It will be as God wills, and no other way. Let me pass. Don't touch me, there is blood on your hands, and blood on your skirts; and you are worse — ten thousand times worse — than any murderer who ever swung on the gallows-tree for her crime! Out of my way, Madame Braelands!"

She stood before him motionless as a white stone with passion, and yet terrified by the righteous anger she had provoked. Words would not come to her, she could not obey his order and move out of his way; so Andrew turned into another path and left her where she stood, for he was impatient of delay, and with steps hurried and stumbling, he followed the husband whom he had driven to his duty.

CHAPTER XII

AMONG HER OWN PEOPLE

BRAELANDS rode like a man possessed, furiously, until he reached the foot of the cliff on which Janet's and Christina's cottages stood. Then he flung the reins to a fisher-laddie, and bounded up the rocky platform. Janet was standing in the door of Christina's cottage talking to the minister. This time she made no opposition to Braelands's entrance; indeed, there was an expression of pity on her face as she moved aside to let him pass.

He went in noiselessly, reverently, suddenly awed by the majesty of Death's presence. This was so palpable and clear, that all the mere material work of the house had been set aside. No table had been laid, no meat cooked; there had been no thought of the usual duties of the day-time. Life stood still to watch the great mystery transpiring in the inner room.

The door to it stood wide open, for the day was hot and windless. Archie went softly in. He fell on his knees by his dying wife, he folded her to his heart, he whispered into her fast-closing ears the despairing words of love, re-awakened, when all repentance was too late. He called her back from the very shoal of time to listen to him. With heart-broken sobs he begged her forgiveness, and she answered him with a smile that had caught the glory of heaven. At that hour he cared not who heard the cry of his agonising love and remorse. Sophy was the whole of his world; and his anguish, so imperative, brought perforce the response of the dying woman who loved him yet so entirely. A few tears — the last she was ever to shed — gathered in her eyes; fondest words of affection were broken on her lips, her last smile was for him, her sweet blue eyes set in death with their gaze fixed on his countenance.

When the sun went down, Sophy's little life of twenty years was over. Her last few hours were very peaceful. The doctor had said she would suffer much; but she did not. Lying in Archie's arms, she slipped quietly out of her clay tabernacle, and doubtless took the way nearest to her Father's House. No one knew the exact moment of her departure — no one but Andrew. He, standing humbly at the foot of her bed, divined by some wondrous instinct the mystic flitting, and so he followed her soul with fervent prayer, and a love which spurned the grave and which was pure enough to venture into His presence with her.

It was a scene and a moment that Archibald Braelands in his wildest and most wretched after-days never forgot. The last rays of the setting sun fell across the death-bed, the wind from the sea came softly through the open window, the murmur of the waves on the sands made a mournful, restless undertone to the majestic words of the minister, who, standing by the bed-side, declared with uplifted hands and in solemnly triumphant tones the confidence and hope of the departing spirit.

"'Lord Thou hast been our dwelling place in all generations.

"' Before the mountains were brought forth, or ever Thou hadst formed the earth and the world ; even from everlasting to everlasting, Thou art God.

"' For a thousand years in Thy sight are but as yesterday when it is past ; and as a watch in the night.

"'The days of our years are three-score years and ten ; and if by reason of strength, they be four-score years, yet is their strength labor and sorrow ; for it is soon cut off, and we fly away.'"

Then there was a pause ; Andrew said " *It is over !* " and Janet took the cold form from the distracted husband, and closed the eyes forever.

There was no more now for Archie to do, and he went out of the room followed by Andrew.

" Thank you for coming for me, Captain," he said, " you did me a kindness I shall never forget."

" I knew you would be glad.   I am grieved to trouble you further, Braelands, at this hour; but the dead must be waited on.   It was Sophy's wish to be buried with her own folk."

" She is my wife."

" Nay, you had taken steps to cast her off."

" She ought to be brought to Braelands."

" She shall never enter Braelands again.   It was a black door to her.   Would you wish hatred and scorn to mock her in her coffin? She bid my mother see that she was buried in peace and good will and laid with her own people."

Archie covered his face with his hands and tried to think.   Not even when dead could he force her into the presence of his mother — and it was true he had begun to cast her off; a funeral from Braelands would be a wrong and an insult.   But all was in confusion in his mind and he said: " I cannot think.   I cannot decide. I am not able for anything more.   Let me go. To-morrow — I will send word — I will come."

" Let it be so then.   I am sorry for you, Braelands — but if I hear nothing further, I will follow out Sophy's wishes."

" You shall hear — but I must have time to

think. I am at the last point. I can bear no more."

Then Andrew went with him down the cliff, and helped him to his saddle; and afterwards he walked along the beach till he came to a lonely spot hid in the rocks, and there he threw himself face downward on the sands, and " communed with his own heart and was still." At this supreme hour, all that was human flitted and faded away, and the primal essence of self was overshadowed by the presence of the Infinite. When the midnight tide flowed, the bitterness of the sorrow was over, and he had reached that serene depth of the soul which enabled him to rise to his feet and say " Thy Will be done ! "

The next day they looked for some communication from Braelands; yet they did not suffer this expectation to interfere with Sophy's explicit wish, and the preparations for her funeral went on without regard to Archie's promise. It was well so, for there was no redemption of it. He did not come again to Pittendurie, and if he sent any message, it was not permitted to reach them. He was notified, however, of the funeral ceremony, which was set for the Sabbath following her death, and Andrew was sure he would at least come for one last look at the wife whom he had loved so much and wronged so deeply. He did not do so.

Shrouded in white, her hands full of white asters, Sophy was laid to rest in the little wind-blown kirkyard of Pittendurie. It was said by some that Braelands watched the funeral from afar off; others declared that he lay in his bed, raving and tossing with fever; but this or that, he was not present at her burial. Her own kin — who were fishers — laid the light coffin on a bier made of oars, and carried it with psalm-singing to the grave. It was Andrew who threw on the coffin the first earth. It was Andrew who pressed the cover of green turf over the small mound, and did the last tender offices that love could offer. Oh, so small a mound! A little child could have stepped over it, and yet, to Andrew, it was wider than all the starry spaces.

The day was a lovely one, and the kirkyard was crowded to see little Sophy join the congregation of the dead. After the ceremony was over, the minister had a good thought; he said: "We will not go back to the kirk; but we will stay here, and around the graves of our friends and kindred praise God for the 'sweet enlargement' of their death." Then he sang the first line of the paraphrase, "O God of Bethel by whose hand," and the people took it from his lips, and made holy songs and words of prayer fill the fresh keen atmosphere, and mingle with the

cries of the sea-birds and the hushed complaining of the rising waters. And that afternoon
many heard for the first time those noble words
from the Book of Wisdom that, during the
more religious days of the middle ages, were
read not only at the grave-side of the beloved,
but also at every anniversary of their death.

" But if the righteous be cut off early by death ; she
shall be at rest.

" For honor standeth not in length of days ; neither
is it computed by number of years.

" She pleased God and was beloved, and she was
taken away from living among sinners.

" Her place was changed, lest evil should mar her
understanding or falsehood beguile her soul.

" She was made perfect in a little while, and finished
the work of many years.

" For her soul pleased God, and therefore He made
haste to lead her forth out of the midst of iniquity.

" And the people saw it and understood it not;
neither considered they this —

" That the grace of God and His mercy are upon
His saints, and His regard unto His Elect."

Chief among the mourners was Sophy's aunt
Griselda. She now bitterly repented the unwise
and unkind " No." Sophy was dearer to her
than she thought, and when she had talked over
her wrongs with Janet, her indignation knew no
bounds. It showed itself first of all to the

author of these wrongs. Madame came early
to her shop on Monday morning, and presum-
ing on her last confidential talk with Miss
Kilgour, began the conversation on that basis.

"You see, Miss Kilgour," she said with a sigh,
"what that poor girl's folly has led her to."

"I see what she has come to. I'm not
blaming Sophy, however."

"Well, whoever is to blame — and I suppose
Braelands should have been more patient with
the troubles he called to himself — I shall have
to put on 'blacks' in consequence. It is a great
expense, and a very useless one; but people
will talk if I do not go into mourning for my
son's wife."

"I wouldn't do it, if I was you."

"Society obliges. You must make me two
gowns at least."

"I will not sew a single stitch for you."

"Not sew for me?"

"Never again; not if you paid me a guinea a
stitch."

"What do you mean? Are you in your
senses?"

"Just as much as poor Sophy was. And
I'll never forgive myself for listening to your
lies about my niece. You ought to be ashamed
of yourself. Your cruelties to her are the talk
of the whole country-side."

" How dare you call me a liar? "

" When I think of wee Sophy in her coffin, I could call you something far worse."

" You are an impertinent woman."

" Ah well, I never broke the Sixth Command. And if I was you, Madame, I would n't put ' blacks ' on about it. But ' blacks ' or no ' blacks,' you can go to some other body to make them for you ; for I want none of your custom, and I 'll be obliged to you to get from under my roof. This is a decent, God-fearing house."

Madame had left before the end of Griselda's orders ; but she followed her to the door, and delivered her last sentence as Madame was stepping into her carriage. She was furious at the truths so uncompromisingly told her, and still more so at the woman who had been their mouthpiece. " A creature whom I have made ! actually made !" she almost screamed. " She would be out at service to-day but for me ! the shameful, impertinent, ungrateful wretch ! "

She ordered Thomas to drive her straight back home, and, quivering with indignation, went to her son's room. He was dressed, but lying prone upon his bed ; his mother's complaining irritated his mood beyond his endurance. He rose up in a passion ; his white haggard face showed how deeply sorrow and remorse had ploughed into his very soul.

" Mother! " he cried, "you will have to hear the truth, in one way or another, from every one. I tell you myself that you are not guiltless of Sophy's death — neither am I."

" It is a lie."

" Do go out of my room. This morning you are unbearable."

" You ought to be ashamed of yourself. Are you going to permit people to insult your mother, right and left, without a word? Have you no sense of honour and decency?"

" No, for I let them insult the sweetest wife ever a man had. I am a brute, a monster, not fit to live. I wish I was lying by Sophy's side. I am ashamed to look either men or women in the face."

" You are simply delirious with the fever you have had."

" Then have some mercy on me. I want to be quiet."

" But I have been grossly insulted."

" We shall have to get used to that, and bear it as we can. We deserve all that can be said of us — or to us." Then he threw himself on his bed again and refused to say another word. Madame scolded and complained and pitied herself, and appealed to God and man against the wrongs she suffered, and finally went into a paroxysm of hysterical weeping. But Archie took no notice of the wordy tempest, so that Madame was confounded and frightened by an indifference so unusual and unnatural.

Weeks of continual sulking or recrimination passed drearily away. Archie, in the first tide of his remorse, fed himself on the miseries which had driven Sophy to her grave. He interviewed the servants and heard all they had to tell him. He had long conversations with Miss Kilgour, and made her describe over and over Sophy's despairing look and manner the morning she ran away. For the poor woman found a sort of comfort in blaming herself and in receiving meekly the hard words Archie could give her. He visited Mrs. Stirling in regard to Sophy's sanity, and heard from that lady a truthful report of all that had passed in her presence. He went frequently to Janet's cottage, and took all her home thrusts and all her scornful words in a manner so humble, so contrite, and so heart-broken, that the kind old woman began finally to forgive and comfort him. And the outcome of all these interviews and conversations Madame had to bear. Her son, in his great sorrow, threw off entirely the yoke of her control. He found his own authority and rather abused it. She had hoped the final catastrophe would draw him closer to her; hoped the coolness of friends and acquaintances would make him more dependent on her love and sympathy. It acted in the opposite direction. The public seldom wants two scapegoats. Madame's ostracism satisfied its idea of justice. Every one knew Archie was very much under her control. Every one could see that he suffered dreadfully after Sophy's death. Every one came promptly to the opinion that Madame only was to blame in the matter. "The poor husband" shared the popular sympathy with Sophy.

However, in the long run, he had his penalty to pay, and the penalty came, as was most just, through Marion Glamis. Madame quickly noticed that after her loss of public respect, Marion's affection grew colder. At the first, she listened to the tragedy of Sophy's illness and death with a decent regard for Madame's feelings on the subject. When Madame poohpoohed the idea of Sophy being in an hospital for weeks, unknown, Marion also thought it "most unlikely;" when Madame was "pretty sure the girl had been in London during the hospital interlude," Marion also thought, "it might be so; Captain Binnie was a very taking man." When Madame said, "Sophy's whole conduct was only excusable on the supposition of her unaccountability," Marion also thought "she did act queerly at times."

Even these admissions were not made with the warmth that Madame expected from Marion, and they gradually grew fainter and more general. She began to visit Braelands less and less frequently, and, when reproached for her remissness, said, "Archie was now a widower, and she did not wish people to think she was running after him;" and her manner was so cold and conventional that Madame could only look at her in amazement. She longed to remind her of their former conversations about Archie, but the words died on her lips. Marion looked quite capable of denying them, and she did not wish to quarrel with her only visitor.

The truth was that Marion had her own designs regarding Archie, and she did not intend Madame to interfere with them. She had made up her mind to marry Braelands, but she was going to have him as the spoil of her own weapons — not as a gift from his mother. And she was not so blinded by hatred as to think Archie could ever be won by the abuse of Sophy. On the contrary, she very cautiously began to talk of her with pity, and even admiration. She fell into all Archie's opinions and moods on the subject, and declared with warmth and positiveness that she had always opposed Madame's extreme measures. In the long run, it came to pass that Archie could talk comfortably with Marion about Sophy, for she always reminded him of some little act of kindness to his wife, or of some instance where he had decidedly taken her part, so that, gradually, she taught him to believe that, after all, he had not been so very much to blame.

In these tactics, Miss Glamis was influenced by the most powerful of motives — self-preservation. She had by no means escaped the public censure, and in that set of society she most desired to please, had been decidedly included in the polite ostracism meted out to Madame. Lovers she had none, and she began to realise, when too late, that the connection of her name with that of Archie Braclands had been a wrong to her matrimonial prospects that it would be hard to remedy. In fact, as the winter went on, she grew hopeless of undoing the odium generated by her friendship with Madame and her flirtation with Madame's son.

"And I shall make no more efforts at conciliation," she said angrily to herself one day, after finding her name had been dropped from Lady Blair's visiting-list; "I will now marry Archie. My fortune and his combined will enable us to live where and how we please. Father must speak to him on the subject at once."

That night she happened to find the Admiral

in an excellent mood for her purpose. The Laird of Binin had not "changed hats" with him when they met on the highway, and he fumed about the circumstance as if it had been a mortal insult.

"I'll never lift my hat to him again, Marion, let alone open my mouth," he cried; "no, not even if we are sitting next to each other at the club dinner. What wrong have I ever done him? Have I ever done him a favour that he should insult me?"

"It is that dreadful Braelands's business. That insolent, selfish, domineering old woman has ruined us socially. I wish I had never seen her face."

"You seemed to be fond enough of her once."

"I never liked her; I now detest her. The way she treated Archie's wife was abominable. There is no doubt of that. Father, I am going to take this situation by the horns of its dilemma. I intend to marry Archie. No one in the county can afford to snub Braelands. He is popular and likely to be more so; he is rich and influential, and I also am rich. Together we may lead public opinion — or defy it. My name has been injured by my friendship with him. Archie Braelands must give me his name."

"By St. Andrew, he shall!" answered the irritable old man. "I will see he does. I ought to have considered this before, Marion. Why did you not show me my duty?"

"It is early enough; it is now only eight months since his wife died."

The next morning as Archie was riding slowly along the highway, the Admiral joined him. "Come home to lunch with me," he said, and Archie turned his horse and went. Marion was particularly sympathetic and charming. She subdued her spirits to his pitch; she took the greatest interest in his new political aspirations; she listened to his plans about the future with smiling approvals, until he said he was thinking of going to the United States for a few months. He wished to study Republicanism on its own ground, and to examine, in their working conditions, several new farming implements and expedients that he thought of introducing. Then Marion rose and left the room. She looked at her father as she did so, and he understood her meaning.

"Braelands," he said, when they were alone, "I have something to say which you must take into your consideration before you leave Scotland. It is about Marion."

"Nothing ill with Marion, I hope?"

"Nothing but what you can cure. She is suffering very much, socially, from the constant association of her name with yours."

"Sir?"

"Allow me to explain. At the time of your sweet little wife's death, Marion was constantly included in the blame laid to Madame Braelands. You know now how unjustly."

"I would rather not have that subject discussed."

"But, by Heaven, it must be discussed! I have, at Marion's desire, said nothing hitherto, because we both saw how much you were suffering; but, sir, if you are going away from Fife, you must remember before you go that the living have claims as well as the dead."

"If Marion has any claim on me, I am here, willing to redeem it."

"'If,' Braelands; it is not a question of 'if.' Marion's name has been injured by its connection with your name. You know the remedy. I expect you to behave like a gentleman in this matter."

"You expect me to marry Marion?"

"Precisely. There is no other effectual way to right her."

"I see Marion in the garden; I will go and speak to her."

"Do, my dear fellow. I should like this affair pleasantly settled."

Marion was sitting on the stone bench round the sun dial. She had a white silk parasol over her head, and her lap was full of apple-blossoms. A pensive air softened her handsome face, and as Archie approached, she looked up with a smile that was very attractive. He sat down at her side and began to finger the pink and white flowers. He was quite aware that he was tampering with his fate as well; but at his very worst, Archie had a certain chivalry about women that only needed to be stirred by a word or a look indicating injustice. He was not keen to perceive; but when once his eyes were opened, he was very keen to feel.

"Marion," he said kindly, taking her hand in his, "have you suffered much for my fault?"

"I have suffered, Archie."

"Why did you not tell me before?"

"You have been so full of trouble. How could I add to it?"

"You have been blamed?"

"Yes, very much."

"There is only one way to right you, Marion; I offer you my name and my hand. Will you take it?"

"A woman wants love. If I thought you could ever love me —"

"We are good friends. You have been my comforter in many miserable hours. I will make no foolish protestations; but you know whether you can trust me. And that we should come to love one another very sincerely is more than likely."

"I *do* love you. Have I not always loved you?"

And this frank avowal was just the incentive Archie required. His heart was hungry for love; he surrendered himself very easily to the charming of affection. Before they returned to the house, the compact was made, and Marion Glamis and Archibald Braelands were definitely betrothed.

As Archie rode home in the gloaming, it astonished him a little to find that he felt a positive satisfaction in the prospect of telling his mother of his engagement — a satisfaction he did not analyze, but which was doubtless compounded of a sense of justice, and of a not very amiable conviction that the justice would not be more agreeable than justice usually is. Indeed, the haste with which he threw himself from his horse and strode into the Braelands's parlour, and the hardly veiled air of defiance with which he muttered as he went, "It's her own doing; let her be satisfied with her work," showed a heart that had accepted rather than chosen its destiny, and that rebelled a little under the constraint.

Madame was sitting alone in the waning light; her son had been away from her all day, and had sent her no excuse for his detention. She was both angry and sorrowful; and there had been a time when Archie would have been all conciliation and regret. That time was past. His mother had forfeited all his respect; there was nothing now between them but that wondrous tie of motherhood which a child must be utterly devoid of grace and feeling to forget. Archie never quite forgot it. In his worst moods he would tell himself, "after all she is my mother. It was because she loved me. Her inhumanity was really jealousy, and jealousy is cruel as the grave." But this purely natural feeling lacked now all the confidence of mutual respect and trust. It was only a natural feeling; it had lost all the nobler qualities springing from a spiritual and intellectual interpretation of their relationship.

"You have been away all day, Archie," Madame complained. "I have been most unhappy about you."

"I have been doing some important business."

"May I ask what it was?"

"I have been wooing a wife."

"And your first wife not eight months in her grave!"

"It was unavoidable. I was in a manner forced to it."

"Forced? The idea! Are you become a coward?"

"Yes," he answered wearily; "anything before a fresh public discussion of my poor Sophy's death."

"Oh! Who is the lady?"

"There is only one lady possible."

"Marion Glamis?"

"I thought you could say 'who'."

"I hope to heaven you will never marry that woman! She is false from head to foot. I would rather see another fisher-girl here than Marion Glamis."

"You yourself have made it impossible for me to marry any one but Marion; though, believe me, if I could find another 'fisher-girl' like Sophy, I would defy everything, and gladly and proudly marry her to-morrow."

"That is understood; you need not reiterate. I see through Miss Glamis now, the deceitful, ungrateful creature!"

"Mother, I am going to marry Miss Glamis. You must teach yourself to speak respectfully of her."

"I hate her worse than I hated Sophy. I

am the most wretched of women;" and her air
of misery was so genuine and hopeless that it
hurt Archie very sensibly.

"I am sorry," he said; "but you, and you
only, are to blame. I have no need to go
over your plans and plots for this very end; I
have no need to remind you how you seasoned
every hour of poor Sophy's life with your
regrets that Marion was *not* my wife. These
circumstances would not have influenced me,
but her name has been mixed up with mine and
smirched in the contact."

"And you will make a woman with a
'smirched' name Mistress of Braelands? Have
you no family pride?"

"I will wrong no woman, if I know it; that
is my pride. If I wrong them, I will right
them. However, I give myself no credit about
righting Marion, her father made me do so."

"My humiliation is complete. I shall die
of shame."

"Oh, no! You will do as I do — make the
best of the affair. You can talk of Marion's
fortune and of her relationship to the Earl of
Glamis, and so on."

"That nasty, bullying old man! And you
to be frightened by him! It is too shameful."

"I was not frightened by him; but I have
dragged one poor innocent woman's name

through the dust and dirt of public discussion, and, before God, Mother, I would rather die than do the same wrong to another. You know the Admiral's temper; once roused to action, he would spare no one, not even his own daughter. It was then my duty to protect her."

"I have nursed a viper, and it has bitten me. To-night I feel as if the bite would be fatal."

"Marion is not a viper; she is only a woman bent on protecting herself. However, I wish you would remember that she is to be your daughter-in-law, and try and meet her on a pleasant basis. Any more scandal about Braelands will compel me to shut up this house absolutely and go abroad to live."

The next day Madame put all her pride and hatred out of sight and went to call on Marion with congratulations; but the girl was not deceived. She gave her the conventional kiss, and said all that it was proper to say; but Madame's overtures were not accepted.

"It is only a flag of truce," thought Madame as she drove homeward, "and after she is married to Archie, it will be war to the knife-hilt between us. I can feel that, and I would not fear it if I was sure of Archie. But alas, he is so changed! He is so changed!'

Marion's thoughts were not more friendly, and she did not scruple to express them in words to her father. "That dreadful old woman was here this afternoon," she said. "She tried to flatter me; she tried to make me believe she was glad I was going to marry Archie. What a consummate old hypocrite she is! I wonder if she thinks I will live in the same house with her?"

"Of course she thinks so."

"I will not. Archie and I have agreed to marry next Christmas. She will move into her own house in time to hold her Christmas there."

"I wouldn't insist on that, Marion. She has lived at Braelands nearly all her life. The Dower House is but a wretched place after it. The street in which it stands has become not only poor, but busy, and the big garden that was round it when the home was settled on her was sold in Archie's father's time, bit by bit, for shops and a preserving factory. You cannot send her to the Dower House."

"She cannot stay at Braelands. She charges the very air of any house she is in with hatred and quarrelling. Every one knows she has saved money; if she does not like the Dower House, she can go to Edinburgh, or London, or anywhere she likes — the further away from Braelands, the better."

CHAPTER XIII

THE " LITTLE SOPHY "

MADAME did not go to the Dower House. Archie was opposed to such a humiliation of the proud woman, and a compromise was made by which she was to occupy the house in Edinburgh which had been the Braelands's residence during a great part of every winter. It was a handsome dwelling, and Madame settled herself there in great splendour and comfort; but she was a wretched woman in spite of her surroundings. She had only unhappy memories of the past; she had no loving anticipations for the future. She knew that her son was likely to be ruled by the woman at his side, and she hoped nothing from Marion Glamis. The big Edinburgh house with its heavy dark furniture, its shadowy draperies, and its stately gloom, became a kind of death chamber in which she slowly went to decay, body and soul.

No one missed her much or long in Largo, and in Edinburgh she found it impossible to gather round herself the company to which she had been wont. Unpleasant rumours somehow clung to her name; no one said much about her, but she was not popular. The fine dwelling in St. George's Square had seen much gay company in its spacious rooms; but Madame found it a hopeless task to re-assemble it. She felt this want of favour keenly, though she need not have altogether blamed herself for it, had she not been so inordinately conscious of her own personality. For Archie had undoubtedly, in previous winters, been the great social attraction. His fine manners, his good nature, his handsome appearance, his wealth, and his importance as a matrimonial venture, had crowded the receptions which Madame believed owed their success to her own tact and influence.

Gradually, however, the truth dawned upon her; and then, in utter disgust, she retired from a world that hardly missed her, and which had long only tolerated her for the accidents of her connections and surroundings. Her disposition for saving grew into a passion; she became miserly in the extreme, and punished herself night and day in order that she might add continually to the pile of hoarded money which Marion afterwards spent with a lavish prodigality. Occasionally her thin, gray face, and her haggard figure wrapped in a black shawl, were seen at the dusty windows of the room she occupied. The rest of the house she closed. The windows were boarded up and the doors padlocked, and yet she lived in constant fear of attacks from thieves on her life for her money. Finally she dismissed her only servant lest she might be in league with such characters; and thus, haunted by terrors of all kinds and by memories she could not destroy, she dragged on for twenty years a life without hope and without love, and died at last with no one but her lawyer and her physician at her side. She had sent for Archie, but he was in Italy, and Marion she did not wish to see. Her last words were uttered to herself. "I have had a poor life!" she moaned with a desperate calmness that was her only expression of the vast and terrible desolation of her heart and soul.

"A poor life," said the lawyer, "and yet she has left twenty-six thousand pounds to her son."

"A poor life, and a most lonely flitting," reiterated her physician with awe and sadness.

However, she herself had no idea when she removed to Edinburgh of leading so "poor a life." She expected to make her house the centre of a certain grave set of her own class and age; she expected Archie to visit her often; she expected to find many new interests to occupy her feelings and thoughts. But she was too old to transplant. Sophy's death and its attending circumstances had taken from her both personally and socially more than she knew. Archie, after his marriage, led entirely by Marion and her ways and desires, never went towards Edinburgh. The wretched old lady soon began to feel herself utterly deserted; and when her anger at this position had driven love out of her heart, she fell an easy prey to the most sordid, miserable, and degrading of passions, the hoarding of money. Nor was it until death opened her eyes that she perceived she had had "a poor life."

She began this Edinburgh phase of it under a great irritation. Knowing that Archie would not marry until Christmas, and that after the marriage he and Marion were going to London until the spring, she saw no reason for her removal from Braelands until their return. Marion had different plans. She induced Archie to sell off the old furniture, and to re-decorate and re-furnish Braelands from garret to cellar. It gave Madame the first profound shock of her new life. The chairs and tables she had used sold at auction to the trades-people of Largo and the farmers of the country·

side! She could not understand how Archie could endure the thought. Under her influence, he never would have endured it; but Archie Braelands smiled on, and coaxed, and sweetly dictated by Marion Glamis, was ready enough to do all that Marion wished.

"Of course the old furniture must be sold," she said. "Why not? It will help to buy the new. We don't keep our old gowns and coats; why then our old chairs and tables?"

"They have associations."

"Nonsense, Archie! So has my white parasol. Shall I keep it in tissue paper forever? Such sentimental ideas are awfully behind the times. Your grandfather's coat and shoes will not dress you to-day; neither, my dear, can his notions and sentiments direct you."

So Braelands was turned, as the country people said, "out of the windows," and Madame hastened away from the sight of such desecration. It made Archie popular, however. The artisans found profitable work in the big rooms, and the county families looked forward to the entertainments they were to enjoy in the renovated mansion. It restored Marion also to general estimation. There was a future before her now which it would be pleasant to share, and every one considered that her engagement to Archie exonerated her from all participation in Madame's cruelty. "She has always declared herself innocent," said the minister's wife, "and Braclands's marriage to her affirms it in the most positive manner. Those who have been unjust to Miss Glamis have now no excuse for their injustice." This authoritative declaration in Marion's favour had such a decided effect that every invitation to her marriage was accepted, and the ceremony, though purposely denuded of everything likely to recall the tragedy now to be forgotten, was really a very splendid private affair.

On the Sabbath before it, Archie took in the early morning a walk to the kirk-yard at Pittendurie. He was going to bid Sophy a last farewell. Henceforward he must try and prevent her memory troubling his life and influencing his moods and motives. It was a cold, chilling morning, and the great immensity of the ocean spread away to the occult shores of the poles. The sky was grey and sombre, the sea cloudy and unquiet; and far off on the eastern horizon, a mysterious portent was slowly rolling onward.

He crossed the stile and walked slowly forward. On his right hand there was a large, newly-made grave with an oar standing upright at its head, and some inscription rudely painted on it. His curiosity was aroused, and he went

306

closer to read the words: "*Be comforted!
Alexander Murray has prevailed.*" The few
words, so full of hope and triumph, moved
him strangely. He remembered the fisherman
Murray, whose victory over death was so certainly announced; and his soul, disregarding all
the forbidding of priests and synods, instantly
sent a prayer after the departed conqueror.
"Wherever he is," he thought, "surely he is
closer to Heaven than I am."

He had been in the kirk-yard often when
none but God saw him, and his feet knew well
the road to Sophy's grave. There was a slender shaft of white marble at the head, and
Andrew Binnie stood looking at it. Braelands
walked forward till only the little green mound
separated them. Their eyes met and filled
with tears. They clasped hands across her
grave and buried every sorrowful memory,
every sense of wrong or blame, in its depth
and height. Andrew turned silently away;
Braelands remained there some minutes longer.
The secret of that invisible communion remained forever his own secret. Those only
who have had similar experiences know that
souls who love each other may, and can, exchange impressions across immensity.

He found Andrew sitting on the stile, gaz-
ing thoughtfully over the sea at the pale grey

wall of inconceivable height which was draw-
ing nearer and nearer. "The fog is coming,"
he said, "we shall soon be going into cloud
after cloud of it."

"They chilled and hurt her once. She is
now beyond them."

"She is in Heaven. God be thanked for His
great mercy to her!"

"If we only knew something *sure*. Where
is Heaven? Who can tell?"

"In Thy presence is fullness of joy, and at
Thy right hand pleasures forevermore. Where
God is, there is Heaven."

"Eye hath not seen, nor ear heard."

"But God *hath* revealed it; not a *future* revelation, Braelands, but a *present* one." And
then Andrew slowly, and with pauses full of
feeling and intelligence, went on to make clear
to Braelands the Present Helper in every time
of need. He quoted mainly from the Bible,
his one source of all knowledge, and his words
had the splendid vagueness of the Hebrew,
and lifted the mind into the illimitable. And
as they talked, the fog enveloped them, one
drift after another passing by in dim majesty,
till the whole world seemed a spectacle of
desolation, and a breath of deadly chillness
forced them to rise and wrap their plaids
closely round them. So they parted at the

kirk-yard gate, and never, never again met in this world.

Braclands turned his face towards Marion and a new life; and Andrew went back to his ship with a new and splendid interest. It began in wondering, "whether there was any good in a man abandoning himself to a noble, but vain regret? Was there no better way to pay a tribute to the beloved dead?" Braclands's costly monument did not realise his conception of this possibility; but as he rowed back to his ship in the gathering storm, a thought came into his mind with all the assertion of a clang of steel, and he cried out to his Inner Man:

"*That*, oh my soul, is what I will do; *that* is what will keep my love's name living and lovely in the hearts of her people."

His project was not one to be accomplished without much labour and self-denial. It would require a great deal of money, and he would have to save with conscientious care many years to compass his desire, which was to build a Mission Ship for the deep sea fishermen. Twelve years he worked and saved, and then the ship was built; a strong steam-launch, able to buffet and bear the North Sea when its waves were running wild over everything. She was provided with all appliances for religious comfort and teaching; she had medicines for the sick and surgical help for the wounded; she carried every necessary protection against the agonising "sea blisters" which torture the fishermen in the winter season. And this vessel of many comforts was called the "Sophy Traill."

She is still busy about her work of mercy. Many other Mission Ships now traverse the great fishing-fleets of the North Sea, and carry hope and comfort to the fishermen who people its grey, wild waters; but none is so well beloved by them as the "Little Sophy." When the boats lie at their nets on a summer's night, it is on the "Little Sophy" that "Rock of Ages" is started and then taken up by the whole fleet. And when the stormy winds of winter blow great guns, then the "Little Sophy," flying her bright colours in the day-time and showing her many lights at night, is always rolling about among the boats, blowing her whistle to tell them she is near by, or sending off help in her lifeboat, or steaming after a smack in distress.

Fifteen years after Andrew and Archie parted at the kirk-yard, Archie came to the knowledge first of Andrew's living monument to the girl they had both loved so much. He was coming from Norway in a yacht with a few friends, and they were caught in a heavy, easterly gale. In a few hours there was a tremendous sea, and the wind rapidly rose to a hurricane. The "Little Sophy" steamed after the helpless craft and got as near to her as possible; but as she lowered her lifeboat, she saw the yacht stagger, stop, and then founder. The tops of her masts seemed to meet, she had broken her back, and the seas flew sheer over her.

The lifeboat picked up three men from her, and one of them was Archie Braelands. He was all but dead from exposure and buffeting; but the surgeon of the Mission Ship brought him back to life.

It was some hours after he had been taken on board; the storm had gone away northward as the sun set. There was the sound of an organ and of psalm-singing in his ears, and yet he knew that he was in a ship on a tossing sea, and he opened his eyes, and asked weakly:

"Where am I?"

The surgeon stooped to him and answered in a cheery voice: "*On the ' Sophy Traill!* '"

A cry, shrill as that of a fainting woman, parted Archie's lips, and he kept muttering in a half-delirious stupor all night long, "*The Sophy Traill! The Sophy Traill!*" In a few days he recovered strength and was able to leave the boat which had been his salvation;

but in those few days he heard and saw much that greatly influenced for the noblest ends his future life.

All through the borders of Fife, people talked of Archie's strange deliverance by this particular ship, and the old story was told over again in a far gentler spirit. Time had softened ill-feeling, and Archie's career was touched with the virtue of the tenderly remembered dead.

"He was but a thoughtless creature before he lost wee Sophy," Janet said, as she discussed the matter; "and now, where will you find a better or a busier man? Fife's proud of him, and Scotland's proud of him, and if England hasn't the sense of discerning *who* she ought to make a Prime Minister of, that isn't Braelands's fault."

"For all that," said Christina, sitting among her boys and girls, "Sophy ought to have married Andrew. She would have been alive today if she had."

"You aren't always an oracle, Christina, and you have a deal to learn yet; but I'm not saying but what poor Sophy did make a mistake in her marriage. Folks should marry in their own class, and in their own faith, and among their own folk, or else ninety-nine times out of a hundred they marry sorrow; but I'm not so sure that being alive to-day would have been a miracle of pleasure and good fortune. If she had had bairns, as ill to bring up and as noisy and fashious as yours are, she is well spared the trouble of them."

"You have spoiled the bairns yourself, Mother. If I ever check or scold them, you are aye sure to take their part."

"Because you never know when a bairn is to blame and when its mother is to blame. I forgot to teach you that lesson."

Christina laughed and said something about it "being a grand thing Andrew had no lads and lasses," and then Janet held her head up proudly, and said with an air of severe admonition:

"It's well enough for you and the like of you to have lads and lasses; but my boy Andrew has a duty far beyond it, he has the 'Sophy Traill' to victual and store, and send out to save souls and bodies."

"Lads and lasses aren't bad things, Mother."

"They'll be all the better for the 'Sophy Traill' and the other boats like her. That laddie o' yours that will be off to sea whether you like it or not, will give you many a fear and heartache. Andrew's 'boat of blessing' goes where she is bid to go, and does as she is told to do. That's the difference."

Difference or not, his "boat of blessing" was Andrew's joy and pride. She had been his salvation, inasmuch as she had consecrated that passion for hoarding money which was the weak side of his character. She had given to his dead love a gracious memory in the hearts of thousands, and "a name far better than that of sons and daughters."

THE END.